The Age of Majority

T.R. Smith

i

ACKNOWLEDGEMENTS

If you were to attempt to write a book yourself one day, I can tell you firsthand, you're going to need help. That said, I am grateful for those that helped, coached, edited, read, calmed me down, and encouraged me along the way. Your efforts mean the world to me.

My resilient, loving, and supportive mother, Linda Ann, who was my first English and writing teacher. Her and her red pen started it all. I love you, Mom!

For having a team of siblings like mine (I'm the baby), who asked many questions, read the first draft and encouraged me the way only siblings know how, I am forever grateful. I love you, Maggie Kladis, Tracey Jagielski and Brandon Smith.

Annie Aldom. The friend who trudged her way through every draft of this book without complaint. From helping with characters' names to answering random emails, she is a true friend, and her hopeful spirit carried me through to the end. Thank you, Annie!

Margot Klima, who read and edited the book before leaving this life too soon. I'm grateful for her professional opinion and what I learned from her about writing and baseball!

Attorney and friend, James M. Brown, who reintroduced me to the 'can-do' attitude. An author himself, James also has become a mentor and trusted advisor. If you hang around James enough, your life begins to improve.

Lastly, I wouldn't be composing this if it weren't for a renewed high school friendship with author, Miles Watson. His advice and raw, honest insight inspired me and showed me what it would take to pull this off. His debut novel, *Cage Life*, continues to win readers over, and I'm grateful to have witnessed him embrace the process. Thank you for the inspiration, Miles.

Miles also introduced me to author, editor, and publisher Michael Dell, who helped take my story to new heights and present it in a way that is much more memorable, while I gained an abundance of knowledge from working with him. Michael is a game-changer for any writer. Thank you, sir.

The cover art is credited to graphic artist and friend, Sandra Cosner. Her depth of knowledge and creativity was just what the book needed. I can't thank her enough for getting involved, teaching me so much, and creating a memorable cover.

I would also like to thank any advanced readers, local libraries and the various coffee shops for the free Wi-Fi and uncomfortable seating. We'll do it again soon.

Table of Contents

This book is dedicated to my late uncle, William Ware, who was quoted as saying, "If you want to run with the big dogs, you've got to learn to piss in the tall weeds."

ACT I

Chapter One

"A man can smile and smile and be a villain."
— Aldous Huxley

The stretch Mercedes pulled under the portico as I tore off a valet ticket and ran to the driver-side door. "Good morning, sir, will you be playing golf today? I can have your clubs sent down to the pro shop."

The aromas of espresso and cedar filled my nose as a stately gent stepped from the car holding a wrapped cigar in his mouth. He looked me over. I was a valet in training at Congressional Country Club, outside D.C., and was working a dayshift. He tilted his head as he looked at me, like he may have known me from somewhere.

"What's your name, son?" he said.

"It's Calvin, sir."

With his hands on his hips, he breathed in the warm late August air. The humid season had all but gone, and a gentle breeze made it a perfect day for golf on one of America's most famous courses.

He took a couple steps toward the hill overlooking the seventeenth hole and spoke to the wind, "Calvin, I'll be needing you to caddie for me today."

"Sir?" I said with confusion. "I'm not a caddie, I'm one of the valets." I pulled his heavy, maroon golf bag from the trunk of his car and set it down.

"Well, today you're a caddie." He took a strong pull from his cigar. "And call me Mr. Gibson."

I looked around for help. "Should I speak to my manager, Mr. Gibson?" I felt like I was being conned.

He approached the French doors of the entrance where two other valets, Mark and Roshan, stood. "How 'bout I speak to him?" Mr. Gibson said. "Meet me at the pro shop in half an hour."

The moment the door shut, Mark bolted over to me and got in my face. "You don't caddie for Gibson when you're a trainee."

I had a balled-up fist ready. "What are you so red-assed about? It's not like I volunteered. You heard the guy."

"You should've told him no."

"Stop bitching and take his clubs downstairs. Or maybe you'd rather go down to the parking lot and settle things." He was maybe five-foot-eight, and I had him by four inches easy. Not to mention I had broken the two-hundred-pound mark the previous year. I was mostly the nice guy, but if I crossed the anger threshold,

I could make quick work of a guy like Mark.

He slipped the bag on his shoulder. "Fucking rookie."

"Easy, Mark," Roshan said. "How was he supposed to know? You'll learn the pecking order soon, Squire. Don't sweat it."

Roshan had become a good friend. I met him at high school, and he was the one who introduced me to valet parking. He even gave me the nickname *Squire*, which had either something to do with social standing or the legendary golfer, Gene Sarazen. Either way, I was okay with it.

I got in and drove the Mercedes through the portico of the Mediterranean style clubhouse and around the circle that enclosed the practice putting green. I passed several of the important members' cars and then took the right turn down to the far parking lot. *Is this Gibson guy serious?* I wouldn't be surprised if it were a prank since I was new at Congressional. That said, I didn't want to jeopardize the best job a high school kid could ever want. I parked the car close to a three-tiered wooden staircase and sprinted up the sixty-seven steps.

With one flight to go, I stopped by the employee cafeteria to quench my thirst. Dan, the valet manager, walked down the hall toward me. "Some guy in a black Mercedes asked me to caddie for him," I said, half out of breath.

"Who?"

"Mr. Gibson."

Dan, a stout fellow with curly brown hair, motioned me to move outside. "Walk with me." This gave me a nervous chill and made me want to apologize. We walked through the service doors toward a row of hedges outside the employee entrance. "Tell me what happened."

"He just got out of his car, looked at me, and told me I was caddying for him."

"You didn't park his car downstairs, did you?"

"I did."

"Calvin, that's Mr. Eli Gibson, and he's what we refer to as a 'five-star member,' so his car stays upstairs. He also doesn't *ask* for anything, he *directs*. Did he give you a tee time?"

"Half an hour at the pro shop."

"Ever caddie before?"

"A few times for my uncle." That was mostly true.

"Good. Don't say much. Rake the bunkers. Keep his clubs clean. And the yardage markers are all to the center of the greens."

I had to get Mr. Gibson's car upstairs in a hurry because I still needed to report to the caddie house, put on a light blue coverall—the Congressional caddie uniform—and grab a couple towels. I had heard that if you looped a bag at Congressional, you could earn up to sixty bucks for a round, sometimes more.

I jumped in the Mercedes and took off down the lot. Mr. Gibson had some file folders on the

4

passenger's seat that began to shift, but when I reached across in a failed attempt to keep them from falling, the steering wheel slipped. I couldn't recover in time, and the heavy car slammed into a wooden post with a 'SLOW' sign attached to it. When I finished cursing, I saw a slew of black and white photographs had spilled from the folders. And these weren't holiday family pictures. They were either porn or some kind of strange fetish. But Gibson's kinks were the least of my worries.

After a few deep breaths, I got out of the Mercedes to assess the damage and to think about what I was going to say to Gibson. We were looking at a new headlamp and possible damage to the front quarter panel, which was the only body part of a car that I knew besides the hood. After getting back in the car, I drove up the hill and parked out of the way of anyone coming or going. I picked up the top two file folders, the bottom one being fully intact. I took one last glance at the photos and worked to put them back as best I could.

I began rehearsing apologies in my mind and tried to factor how many sprints up the stairs it would take to cover the damage to the car. That was assuming I still had a job.

***

The sun played hide and seek behind cotton white clouds over the course, causing shadows that seemed to chase each other. A half hour had easily gone by while I waited outside the pro shop, seated on a bench. Still no Mr. Gibson. The knot in my stomach would only go away if I fessed up, and then the inevitable guilt could run its course. I kept thinking about the photos, particularly a provocative young woman who was involved in some sexual deviance I had never even seen in a magazine.

A few looks of disapproval came my way from the caddie house; they must have heard about the arrangements. When I stood up from the steel bench to stretch, Gibson happened to be walking through the pro shop.

Pushing the door open, he said, "little quiet for a Saturday." He was holding a large foam cup, no doubt a cocktail. He wore yellow slacks and a blue golf shirt with a logo from *Winged Foot Golf Club* on the left chest.

"I doubt for long," I said. "School started. Maybe families are settling in."

"You in school?" He threw his foot up on the bench to retie one of his golf shoes, his metal spikes scraping the concrete.

"Yes, sir. I'm a senior at Whitman."

"Walt Whitman. Great writer. You like it there?"

"It's a lot different than my old school. I just moved here from Ohio, outside Cleveland." He began walking toward the tenth tee box. I looked back at the caddie house and wondered if I had forgotten anything, like setting up his tee time.

"Mr. Gibson, are we starting on the back nine?" I flung the heavy golf bag over my shoulder and ran to catch up.

"Only time for nine holes today I'm afraid."

"Should I inform the starter then?"

"Don't bother," he said. "They know."

At the tee box, he asked for the three-wood. I handed him his club. I remembered what my boss had told me, *Don't say much*, so I tried to remain quiet, which wasn't easy for me.

"My friend, Gabe Fleming from ABC, had to cancel," Gibson said. "Otherwise, it would've been eighteen."

I was floored. *Gabe Fleming? The national news anchorman?* I couldn't believe it. We marched on without the famed Mr. Fleming, down the most pristine and perfectly manicured grounds that I'd ever walked. I no longer cared about the money after seeing this place up close. Okay, maybe I still cared for the girl in the photograph, but I was sharing turf with Eisenhower, JFK, Palmer, and Nicklaus. My aspirations for politics would include rounds of golf someday, and they would happen right here at Congressional. After I took the oath of office, of course.

Mr. Gibson showed to be a good golfer, which was no surprise since he was built like one: medium height, light in weight, and thin arms and chest, ideal for swinging a club. However, he did display an explosive temper. On more than one occasion, after a bad shot, he turned red in the face and screamed, "Damn it!" He also complained about unlucky bounces—something us golfers call *the rub of the green*.

I watched him closely and tried to guess his profession. I ruled out doctor or engineer since his temperament didn't match those. He had a roughness, as well as a cunning nature, about him. He had to be either a lawyer or a businessman, especially considering his ego. Whatever he did, it was on a large scale, or that's how I felt around him.

He was a big shot.

He lit another dark cigar and plotted himself around the course with fine skills. He would hand me the cigar while he putted on Congressional's large, undulating greens. I let the smoke linger into my nose, and it smelled wonderful. The label read *Partagas*.

After his final putt on the eighteenth hole, I replaced the flagstick, and we shook hands.

"You're not bad," he said.

"Thanks, Mr. Gibson. I enjoyed it." Thoughts of the car started creeping back.

"Good. We'll do it again."

No, we probably won't. "Look, Mr. Gibson. We have to settle something."

He laughed and put a hand on my shoulder. "I know I owe you some money, but we haven't even walked off the green yet."

"No, I owe you money."

"You've lost me, son."

"Why did you want me to caddie for you today?"

"Because you seem like a nice young man. You remind me of someone...and I figured you would enjoy the experience. Now, what's this about?"

I picked up the golf bag and stood it straight. "For some reason, me caddying for you pissed off a few people, and then I got all rattled and wrecked your Mercedes."

Mr. Gibson paused and looked at me like maybe I was bluffing. "And you waited until now to tell me?"

"Sir, I didn't want to ruin your game. I've already made plans to get the car fixed. It's a headlamp and maybe a little body work. I can't tell you how sorry I am."

I had a quick revelation that no matter what he chose to do, if I followed through on my word and fixed his car, he would always remember me. *Maybe this is an opportunity.*

He put his glove and divot tool away in his bag and snickered as he looked out over the green. "The most powerful people in this town know not to fuck with me, and I get played by a varsity letterman."

"I'm not playing you, Mr. Gibson."

"No? Ok, then. How do we make this right? The club has insurance, but that means we'd have to tell your boss."

"I'll fix the car."

"This could actually work out for both of us."

"Sir?"

"If I report it, you're out of luck. But since I need a favor…." He squinted as if in thought. "It looks like you work for me now." I immediately thought of the photographs. He pulled a money clip from the golf bag and flipped me a crisp hundred-dollar bill. I looked back at the golf course thinking *What the hell just happened?* With that, I grabbed the golf bag and followed my new boss up the hill.

And that's how I met Eli Gibson.

Chapter Two

"Best lamb chops in the city right here," Mr. Gibson said, as he got out of the car—his brand-new black Toyota Supra Turbo. He snatched the ticket from the valet without saying a word. We had driven into the city, down into the Farragut Square neighborhood to the Dolley Madison Hotel. The neighborhood is in Northwest Washington and is home to a lot of legal and media offices, the Army Navy Club, and Constitution Hall. The maître d' knew Mr. Gibson and gave him a modest welcome when we reached the front desk.

In the foyer of the Dolley Madison, facing us, was quite possibly the most beautiful young woman I'd ever seen in my life. She had flowing, dark hair that she brushed to one side. She was wearing a mid-length red dress with a black buckle. Mr. Gibson approached her with a sly little kiss on her cheek, which she didn't seem too excited about. She was all business—I liked that about her.

Mr. Gibson said, "Say hello to the future of public relations, Calvin. This is Nora Dalton." She was an absolute knockout. Perhaps a little older than me, her eyes were an interesting shade of brown—not quite like almonds, more like cognac. Her nail polish and lipstick matched her dress, and without her heels, she was probably close to five-foot-seven.

"Hello, Miss Dalton. I'm Calvin Ducane."

We shook hands, and she gave me a smile. "Don't you know what you're getting into?" They both laughed. Mr. Gibson walked over to the front desk to read the wine list with the maître d'.

"Anything interesting happening in your life, Calvin?" Nora asked.

Now there is. "Spending my last year of high school in Washington, during an election year. I'm just looking to stay out of trouble."

"If you're dining with us, you're not off to a good start." What a style and grace about her. The tiniest touch of smoke in her voice. Somewhere along the way, there had to be some Southern roots because of her charming manner and elegant drawl. She stood close to me for a moment to let someone walk by, allowing a slight whiff of her perfume. Fresh flowers, maybe ocean water. And yet her best features and qualities were hidden behind a commitment to being simple. She refused to show off or draw any unwanted attention.

The maître d' walked us to a table with a window view. My night had just got a lot more interesting.

Mr. Gibson ordered a bottle of French Bordeaux—three hundred dollars on the wine list, he told us. That certainly piqued my interest, even if he were showing off. I felt uncomfortable and wanted to undo the collar on my dress shirt but tried to ignore it. As I studied the table setting, I couldn't help but notice a polished glass vase. I picked it up.

"What's this?"

"Fine wine needs to breathe, son," Mr. Gibson said. "It's called a decanter."

"You like wine, Calvin?" Nora said.

"I would have to say yes, even though I don't know a lot about it."

"Well, you've got your whole life to become a wine snob, so be careful."

"Or argue about it like she and I do," Mr. Gibson said.

A slender waiter came back with the bottle and presented it to Mr. Gibson, who yanked the decanter from the waiter's hands and filled the glasses himself, spilling some as he went along. Nora swatted him and said something under her breath. I picked up the bottle and read its label.

"Bordeaux," Mr. Gibson said, as the waiter scurried off.

I mimicked Mr. Gibson and gave the wine a good sniff before taking a sip. Nora smiled when I did this, which made me blush.

The wine was odd. I wasn't disappointed or anything, it was just different. Complex, I guess. A while later, after courses of escargot and Caesar salad, the waiter brought our dinner, which was rack of lamb. The lamb was rare and sat in a pool of rich, dark brown sauce. "This is incredible," I said. "I've never had rack of lamb."

He took a mouthful of it and put his knife and fork down. He picked up his wine glass and leaned toward me. "Stick with us, and you'll be eating a lot of it."

"Well, can we talk about this work arrangement?"

"Oh, heaven forbid, Eli," Nora said. She placed her wine glass on the table. "What did he tell you, Calvin?"

"He wrecked my car," Mr. Gibson said. "I'd say he's into me for a couple of dimes." He placed his napkin on the table and stood up. A tall, white-haired gentleman approached our table, and they exchanged a handshake and a half hug. It was Donald Gallagher, the current Speaker of the House.

I watched the two of them. I was just a kid, but I had some street smarts. Something didn't add up. I just happen to resemble someone and that's why I've been his caddie and his dinner guest. The guy drives around with voyeur-like photos in his car, and now he's hugging the third-most-powerful person in the country. I did the formal meet-and-greet with the Speaker and waited to sit back down.

"Know who that was?" Nora said.

"The man with the gavel, Mr. Gallagher," I said.

"Ahh, not bad for public school," Mr. Gibson said as Nora nodded her head. His remark gave me the

14

urge to bring up my Uncle Jack, who had been in the Senate for the past thirteen years and was a former governor, but I wasn't there to play *who's who.*

"I try to read the front page every day," I said.

Mr. Gibson shot glares at the waiter and made frequent demands, prompting Nora to correct his questionable manners more than once. I felt the urge to apologize to the waiter on Mr. Gibson's behalf but couldn't find the opportunity.

"Is he always this. . ." I whispered to Nora.

"This much of a jerk?" Nora said out loud. "Not usually, but I've seen him act worse."

I noticed him using the tablecloth to spin the base of his wine glass in a clockwise manner. From what I could tell, the man liked his booze. "Good, no?" he said.

After taking a sip, I thought for a second. "Yeah. It's wicked."

He laughed. "Wicked? A wicked Bordeaux."

Nora tried not to roll her eyes.

There weren't many people left in the room, as the dinner hour had passed. Our table faced Fifteenth Street, and the night's traffic slowly died down. Rows of dim lamps atop pearl-colored tablecloths made for a swanky room. The last two remaining servers dressed each table to perfection with flatware and polished wine glasses. The tall windows had full-length, bronze-colored drapes framing views of the city. From where I sat, I couldn't see any of the monuments or the Capitol, which was a shame. The Capitol was spectacular, and whenever in the city, I always looked for it.

After finishing dessert, something Mr. Gibson had introduced as *pot de crème*, I watched him scribble in a tip and sign the check. Every detail of his clothing, down to the cashmere sport coat and the gold Rolex, were top of the line. But why did he have to be so arrogant and rude?

I stood up as Nora rose to use the ladies' room.

"Why, you've got some Southern roots, Calvin?"

"Mom's side crossed the Mason-Dixon a while back, but I'm a Buckeye at heart." It was customary in my family for men to stand up when a woman enters a room or gets up to use the ladies' room.

Mr. Gibson watched what I had done and nodded his head, though he seemed more interested in the wine.

Once I had finished watching Nora leave, I said, "Mr. Gibson, what do you do for a living?"

"I build relationships." He placed his empty wine glass on the table. "People call me a *power broker*."

A broker in Washington had to mean that he was some sort of lobbyist. At least that was my best guess. And since he hugs the Speaker of the House in public, I suppose he's a powerful one. Right then and there, I had forgotten all about trying to adjust to my new school and my boring living arrangements. I wanted to see more of this lifestyle. I wanted to understand Eli Gibson.

Nora returned, and Mr. Gibson was suddenly in a rush.

"Are you trying to ditch me again, Eli?" Nora said.

"I have a nine o'clock tomorrow, will you be free after that? Need to go over some things. I think Calvin here will be a good fit, don't you?"

Nora ran her arm along my back and looked at me. It gave me the chills. Her eyes were calm and soothing from the wine and probably a long day. "Something about him seems to be a good fit."

Mr. Gibson threw his embroidered napkin down on his dessert plate and walked hastily through the dining room. "You'd better go," she said. It was all I could do to keep pace with him.

"Good night, Mr. Gibson," the maître d' said.

Mr. Gibson ignored him and looked at me. "Wait here," he said. He walked up the few carpeted stairs toward the men's room, so I turned and faced the front desk.

"I apologize for any annoyance."

The maître d' wore a black tuxedo with slick black hair and eyes dark enough to match. He was putting away wine lists and menus and glanced at me. "He's probably got a lot on his mind right now."

Nora had entered the foyer. "You're right about that, Miguel," she said. More small talk ensued.

"Always a pleasure, Miss Nora. Thank you for dining at the Dolley Madison."

"I take it you're not coming with us," I said to Nora.

"My work beckons," she said. "But I'll see you soon. Eli wants to get you in the mix. It was so nice meeting you, Calvin."

I watched the bellhop open the glass door for her, and she walked outside to a waiting BMW.

***

Mr. Gibson and I walked out to the front of the hotel and waited for the valet. He looked down the street. "Can't trust any of these kids…out joyriding, I'll bet."

"Does that go for Congressional valets also?" I unwrapped a mint and took in the warm air. *I'd be out joyriding too, if it were me.*

That night, we were driving for sport. The Supra was a 1987 Turbo—barely a hundred miles on it. By no means a Ferrari, the Supra still a beautiful sports car, and fast. Painted jet black and complete with 230 horsepower, it had tires that could chew the pavement on Washington's tight turns and winding streets. That night was perfect for it—summer, warm, and not much humidity, ideal driving weather.

Mr. Gibson brushed off the valet like he did most people in the service industry: nose up in the air, handing off a five-dollar bill with no thank you. For a moment, I thought it might be fun to be a valet downtown as opposed to a country club, especially living in Washington, but if I had to cater to guys like Eli Gibson, it might be short-lived. I was beginning not to like him, but there was that mysterious side of him that I wanted to figure out. I was intrigued. Meeting Nora was what ultimately made me commit. If any of my time spent with Mr. Gibson involved her, then you didn't have to tell me twice. And then there was that favor I owed him.

We left the Dolley Madison, and he hit the throttle hard. I wasn't expecting it, so I laughed to cover up being nervous. He drove south on Fifteenth toward the middle of the city. This is where Washington shows her true beauty, especially at night. I believe he made a point to drive down one of the most famous stretches of road—Pennsylvania Avenue.

"Been to driving school?" I said. The scream of the engine caused us to yell.

"You have no idea, son." He glanced over at me. "Scared, are you?"

He was indifferent. Here was a guy who looks like he has it all, but for some reason, he feels the need to belittle restaurant workers and show off for a seventeen-year-old. I guessed that he was probably a lousy poker player.

The White House came into view, and he rolled down his window. He pointed toward the wrought iron fence. "And I've got the keys to that house right there." He looked back at me with a frenzied glare and yelled, "What do you think of that?"

Bullshit.

He took the Supra near the curb to pass another car. "Do you even know who I am, son?"

I didn't like him calling me "son."

"I'm skilled at driving in terrorism," he said. "Learned it in Vietnam." With a swift jerk of the wheel, he moved into oncoming traffic and laid on the gas. With one hand on the horn and the other on the headlamp switch, he made himself known to the other motorists.

"If someone wants to kill you, this is how you escape!"

He drove in a zig-zag pattern, causing the tires to screech every other second as the car spun around like it might tip over. The Supra lunged in and out of oncoming traffic. I remember seeing flashes of streetlights, headlights and lit-up buildings. I could smell the rubber from the tires. I clung to the seat, and he glanced at me, driving even faster and more erratic.

Horns blared from other motorists. He pulled in a breath, his face beet-red. "If we escaped an embassy bombing, this is how we'd do it!"

"All right, all right, I get it!" Now, on top of his quirks, he was also dangerous, and I wasn't sure how I felt about it.

Once his tirade was over, he brought the car back onto the proper side of the road and took Connecticut Avenue to the Kalorama neighborhood. He parked on a residential street and faced me. I caught a faint whiff of that cologne again. I wasn't a big cologne guy, but I had to know the name of that one. The five times a year that I might wear it, I wanted it to be that one. It had scents of leather, deep forest, and sandalwood.

"I was a foreign news correspondent in Vietnam," he said in what felt like a rehearsed lecture. "After some differences with CBS News, I moved to Tokyo, where I became involved in the political arena. After six years of lobbying there, I moved to D.C. to lobby on behalf of Japanese businessmen and government officials. Some of Washington's most powerful sought my services. They all wanted a piece of Eli Gibson. Still do, to be honest. And all I need to do, son…is hang a lamb chop in the window."

His words froze me for a second. "A lamb chop?"

"That's right, son. Just like Perle used to say. For all those greedy fuckers."

"Could you please stop calling me 'son'?" He didn't respond. "And who's Perle?"

I'll never forget that night. He stared into the rearview mirror and scratched his stubbled beard. Mr. Gibson gave me a menacing feeling about Washington. And what was his interest in me? Whoever he had spoken about as being greedy fuckers, well, I felt like I had already met some of them, and it didn't help that we had just eaten lamb chops.

Chapter Three

"Where do you live, son?" Mr. Gibson said.

"My grandmother has a place at the Foxhall," I said. "We're staying with her until we get settled."

"I have a place at the Foxhall too. Let's go grab a nightcap."

I looked into his cutting blue eyes. The invitation came off as genuine, so I didn't hesitate. "All right."

He had Carl, one of the Foxhall security employees, meet us at the front entrance and take the car down to the garage. And when I got out of the car, I felt the same importance he liked to display everywhere he went. *Mr. Gibson is here.*

"Good evening, Mr. Gibson," Foxhall's front desk secretary said as we walked in. Her name was Fran. The entrance was too gaudy for my liking, but the Foxhall residents probably approved, especially the attention they received when they entered. I know my grandma loved it. We stopped inside the lobby under the large, antique glass chandelier. Fran looked over her reading glasses at me like she was sizing me up.

"Hi, Fran," I said. Mr. Gibson didn't say hello. Fran kept her eyes on him for a moment, then turned away, shaking her head.

The bellhop, Josh—a guy from Barbados, about twenty, always sporting a huge smile—was there to walk us to the elevator. He looked down the first-floor hallway with surprise, as if to say, *Don't you live in 104?* Just a couple months prior, I was living in a rust-belt town, in a house that a century before served as a barn. Even with the effects that Washington's prestige and excitement can have on someone, I hadn't changed much, but the city was starting to grow on me.

"How you doing, Calvin?" Josh said. He looked at both me and Mr. Gibson twice, as we waited for the elevator. He was caught up in thought, like he couldn't put something together.

"Pretty exciting night," I said to Josh.

The elevators were centered on the back wall of the lobby. There were dark wood chair railings with white and gold striped wallpaper surrounding the foyer. Maroon and forest green carpet in a Persian design ran down the opposite hallways. The floor of the lobby was marble. That, coupled with the arched ceiling, created a substantial echo.

The lobby staff saw a lot of me, considering my love of elevators and my frequent trips up to the roof to look out at the Jefferson Memorial and have a quick smoke. The roof was my refuge. I was searching for something off in the distance, anything, a sign from God, I guess.

As the elevator closed, I watched Fran take a call and Josh walk back to the entrance—it gave me a phony sense of importance, like I was going places. I wanted to do something great, and Washington made me feel that way. The problem was, I had no plan, I was just letting things happen. So far, I was a product of serendipity. Maybe someone like Mr. Gibson would discover my gift of gab and decent manners and help me put them to use. Those traits went a long way in a city like D.C. Of course, an education and possibly some military experience would help.

***

There was a mirror in the condo that took up one side of the living room, making the room look larger than it was. There were several wingback chairs, an overstuffed leather loveseat, and an eight-seat, mahogany dining room table just off the living room. The other walls held elaborate pieces of framed French art.

"Nice place," I said.

"Eh, it's a dump, but I like Foxhall, and my guests like the amenities." He threw his coat on one of the chairs. "Let's have a drink."

We walked into his office. Half the room was mirrored, just like the living room. On the other side of the doorway was a glass cabinet with a ritzy wet bar setup: scotch, gin, vodka, vermouth, and all the trimmings.

"You a gin guy, Calvin?"

"No stranger to gin." He filled two glasses with ice from a bucket and poured two drinks—I could hear the fizz of the tonic water as it flowed over the ice, causing the cubes to rattle.

"So, you're living with your grandma, are you?" he asked as he handed me a drink.

"Yes, sir, great lady. She's been at Foxhall for several years, so I've been here before." Mr. Gibson walked around his desk and sat down. His office chair matched the desk: heavy, dark, luxurious. I could hear the leather as he leaned back. I thought to myself how I'd like to have a setup like that for myself one day.

"Senior year?"

"Yeah, but they gave me the run around. I guess I have to register as a junior, it's complicated."

"Sounds like it."

"I came from a Catholic school, where they taught religion. I guess Maryland public schools don't acknowledge religious studies. No love for baby Jesus."

He laughed. "Gives you time to get settled, I guess."

After more small talk, Mr. Gibson went into how he's "made millions" and how a few years back he had "brokered a big deal with the Japanese," and that's how he landed in Washington. He had my full attention, but I found it odd that he had to boast about it. I was raised to let accomplishments and experiences speak for themselves.

26

I stared into my empty glass. "You mind?" I motioned to the bar.

"Be my guest."

After pouring another drink, we got on the subject of West Point, which was, at the time, more fantasy than reality. My grades were all over the place coming into Whitman, and they weren't improving; hardly what a service academy would be looking for in a future cadet. It was strange—he made it sound like he could just flick a switch and get me in there. Even stranger, I believed him. I'd been there about a half hour after our dinner and wild driving adventure. My mom was probably wondering where the hell I was.

"I need to make a quick call, if that's alright."

"There's a phone right behind you." There was a silver phone on the wall next to the bar. I picked it up to call my grandma's condo. Sure enough, she answered the phone.

"Hello," she said in her raspy, Southern voice.

"Hi, Grandma."

"Well, where the hell are you?" My grandma had a mouth on her in private.

"I met one of our neighbors. Is my mom there?" She was there, probably had one foot in bed already. She grabbed the other phone upstairs.

"Where are you calling from, young man?"

"I met one of our neighbors when I was outside. I'll be home in a bit."

"You'll be home *pronto*, Calvin. It's a school night." The line went dead.

I sat back down and went to work on the last of my gin and tonic, which, in addition to the wine, had started to take effect. I didn't know why my mom was in such an uproar. I had told her that I was working and would've been home at the same time anyway, unless she knew I was lying. I figured this much, if I were to spend any more time with Mr. Gibson, I'd have to be sly about it. I could just sense that she wouldn't approve.

Mr. Gibson stood behind his desk, admiring his pictures and awards. "You in trouble?"

"Nah. But you know how parents are." He didn't respond. I noticed the college diploma on a glass shelf behind him. *Syracuse*.

"A New Yorker?" I said.

"You bet I am." He came off like that: brash, stylish, and a touch pompous. New Yorkers were all in a rat race, and they loved to compete with Washington. It was like he was there as a spy or something—or maybe that was the gin talking. On a shelf above the bar were more pictures: one with him posing with former Secretary of Defense Caspar Weinberger and another with a group of Japanese officials and President Reagan in the Rose Garden. At the end of the shelf were two photos of a young man in a brass-hinged frame. We could have passed for twins.

28

I took the last sip off my marinated lime and said my thanks and good night. Mr. Gibson nodded his head and smiled. "Good night."

Having someone to shoot the breeze with and a liquor cabinet to raid—it had the makings for an interesting working relationship. Looking back, the intensity of the drive down Pennsylvania Avenue seemed more like a thrill ride than a scare tactic. Maybe he wanted to see if I'd go along. Well, I did.

I walked down the long hall to the elevators with a nice buzz. I watched the design on the carpet sway back and forth. I wondered if my new, mysterious friend would go back to his home in Kalorama or stay there that night.

What a nice option to have.

I listened to the city from the rooftop, letting small clouds of smoke leave my mouth. The Jefferson Memorial stood lucid in the dark. The columns and dome were reflecting off the Tidal Basin, but I could barely make it out from where I was. Its beauty, especially from such a distance, was awe-inspiring. Things were falling into place for me, probably faster than they should. I was ready though. I could handle whatever came my way.

I could, couldn't I?

Chapter Four

I changed into my work gear outside my car and took a breath mint. I few questions would no doubt be thrown at me when I walked in.

"Who the hell is this neighbor?" my mom said, as loud as a school bus driver.

We were standing in the foyer of the condo. The stairs that led to the second floor were just off to my left, where my grandma stood, half naked. She had a habit of that. Peering down at me with a quizzical look, she was no doubt jealous that I was out with our swanky neighbor and she wasn't. She kept a curiosity about her neighbors because she was forever looking to build on her audience. I suppose she had every right to, as she accomplished quite a bit in her life, and she'd be goddamned if somebody wasn't going to hear about it. "Well, who is he?" she said.

"I came home from work and went for a walk. I met him out front." Mr. Gibson being a member at Congressional could wait. I didn't want these two ladies connecting any dots. "We went and looked at some pictures in his office. He's a big political—"

"I don't care if he's the *head honcho*, son," my mother said. "It's a school night." 'Head honcho' was a term in our home that was reserved for serious conversations only.

I had to think fast and say little. If either of them were to smell the gin on my breath, I'd need a good lawyer. It's not like I did anything wrong— minus the boozing—so I decided I'd blame most of it on losing track of time. Usually, I'll fess up when I do something terrible, but a little white lie like this wasn't going to hurt anyone. So, with all my confidence, I put this one together:

"Mr. Gibson is a former ABC news correspondent who worked in Vietnam. He is currently lobbying on behalf of the Japanese government. We hit it off right away. He thinks he might be able to help me get into a good school—maybe even West Point. I figure if I can really excel in the classroom, maybe between him and Uncle Jack, there is an outside chance I could make it happen."

Game. Set. Match.

***

A while later, I ran into Mr. Gibson in the roundabout outside the Foxhall. He was dressed in a suit and about to get into his stretch Mercedes Benz, but he wasn't the driver. He looked dapper. He was headed somewhere to work a room, no doubt.

There were two chauffeurs and a couple of other well-dressed gentlemen, one that looked close to my age. I figured he was probably family or something. There were two other cars as well — another stretch Mercedes and an Audi Quattro.

This was some scene in front of Foxhall. I pictured myself getting into that car someday, going downtown to negotiate with some big political figure.

Mr. Gibson tipped his hat. "Stop at the house later, having some friends over."

"Sure thing," I said as I watched his entourage get in their cars.

He leaned into the Mercedes, and, one by one, the car doors slammed shut. The vehicles rounded the circle and drove down the hill, three sets of brake lights flashing in a row.

That evening after dinner, I wondered what I might be missing in Kalorama. I decided to take a drive. I yelled upstairs to my mom, "Hey, I got called into work. They're short a couple valets."

"I never heard the phone ring," she said.

"I have to fill in and work a large party, no big deal." I waited during her usual delay with my head in my hands.

"Are you taking my car?"

"I need to get there as soon as possible, so yeah. Probably get something to eat afterwards then be home."

On the drive over, I couldn't help but wonder if Nora would be there. I parked a block away and gave the Kalorama neighborhood a quick study. I tried to imagine what it would be like to live where Woodrow Wilson or FDR once called home. The houses were built to last, and they all seemed to have inviting entrances, screened-in porches, stone facades, and brick walkways.

When I approached the door, I anticipated Mr. Gibson's butler. Instead, a welcoming scent of perfume greeted me. It smelled the way a summer field would, with fresh flowers and honey. I didn't have the courage to knock. I stood there trying to get the visions of Nora out of my head.

I went ahead and let myself in. I could hear people chatting, and the slight *pop* of a wine bottle being opened. Mr. Gibson was speaking, and by his tone, he sounded like he was enjoying himself. I could hear glasses and plates, flatware and laughter. I relaxed and continued to take in the sounds: wine being poured, background music, and what I thought was possibly the sound of someone snorting cocaine.

I thought about starting over and ringing the doorbell, but he was expecting me, so whatever was happening in his home, he didn't care to hide it from me.

"Hello there." A voice came from the dining room, just past the stairwell. *Nora.*

Goosebumps. "Hey there," I said. "I hope I'm not interrupting." She was seated at the head of the table, alone, with a pile of file folders, an adding machine, and a leather ledger that she was working on under a banker's lamp.

"I'm sure he's expecting you. Let me go grab him." She wore a white, glittered cutaway skirt that sparkled as she walked. Her sleeveless maroon blouse accentuated her, I was guessing, swimmer's frame.

By then, I was standing in the dining room, not sure where to place myself. I felt like I'd broken in or something. I could hear the click of Nora's shoes, and shadows entered the room just as my thoughts were running dry.

"Do you always show up fashionably late, son?" Mr. Gibson said as Nora took her seat and began working again. She didn't pay me much mind.

"Funny. Family dinners usually include some form of interrogation." I caught a look from Nora. I couldn't tell if she were curious or slightly annoyed.

Mr. Gibson relit a cigar. "Pressed for time?"

"My night's wide open."

"Good," he said. "Tonight's the night. Isn't that right, Miss Dalton?"

Nora peered from behind the small, green lamp and let out a sigh. "I suppose it is, Eli."

Mr. Gibson and I joined his guests in the living room for cocktails, at least they were drinking. I wasn't denying being seventeen—at least for another week— and I didn't want to put Mr. Gibson in a predicament.

"Calvin." I heard my name coming from the dining room. I walked the hall to where Nora was seated. To my enjoyment, she was in the middle of stretching her toned back and arms. If she were trying to tease me, it was working. I pretended not to notice as best I could.

"Call for me?"

"Do me a favor and pour me a glass of chardonnay from the bar." If red velvet cake had a voice, it would sound like Nora Dalton. Sultry and confident.

"Sure thing." I began to walk toward the great room when I turned around. "Nora, I usually cocktail with Mr. Gibson, but I don't know anyone else out there. Think anyone would mind my indulging?"

"Considering where we're going tonight, I would almost encourage it."

Chapter Five

It was close to midnight. At least a dozen of us: diplomats, bureaucrats, media types, Nora, myself, and our host, Mr. Gibson. We were riding in a limo-bus that political parties tend to use for campaigning. We were headed downtown.

After a ten-minute drive from Kalorama, we were outside the northwest gate of America's most famous address—1600 Pennsylvania Avenue.

Mr. Gibson stepped off the bus at the gate and spoke to two armed guards, one that he seemed to know personally based on the manner of their conversation. I couldn't make out what they said, but they got along like old pals, shaking hands and sharing a quick joke—I may have even seen the passing of an envelope. The guard walked back to the guardhouse and made a call.

I was seated next to a diplomat from El Salvador, Roman Lynch was his name. "Safe to say this'll be your first tour?" he said.

"You mean there'll be more?"

This caused several on the bus to laugh, including Nora.

Mr. Gibson jumped back inside. "Perfect night for a visit, I'd say." This was as excited as I'd seen him.

There was more to this visit. There had to be. And the fact that no one spoke of it until we arrived made me think that they wanted to see how I would react.

The gates opened, and the bus driver took his time driving the semi-circle up toward the North Lawn. The fountain was lit up and flowed effortlessly, and the grounds were pristine, even in the midnight hour. Later, I discovered that we didn't come in where the public tours took place, but rather, where the guests of state dinners and other officials arrived.

The driver pulled up under the West Wing portico where a White House official greeted us. A Marine in full dress stood guard at the entrance, the Presidential Seal above the doorway. As we exited the limo-bus, the official and Nora joined hands, and she gave him a peck on the cheek. He and Mr. Gibson shook hands with familiarity, and the rest of us followed in a pseudo-receiving line.

I took an interest in politics at a young age, mostly from knowing the senator from my home state was friends with my great-uncle and was also a war hero. This led me to ask permission more than once to sit in the senate chamber balcony and watch my Uncle Jack. And now I was within shouting distance of the president himself, all because I wrecked some lobbyist's car. The chances we take in life, and the things we wish for, sometimes evolve without us even realizing it. I guess that goes back to the notion of serendipity. I heard once at the dinner table that you are the sum of your choices. It makes sense. Did I choose to be at the White House that night? I suppose I did, in a roundabout way.

After entering the lobby of the West Wing, we were welcomed by another White House official. She went right into describing some of the art and explaining the room's history when Nora leaned into me and whispered, "Welcome to the big time, Calvin." I had nothing to say. *Boy, if they could see me now.*

As a group, everyone was loose and courteous, but there was eagerness in their voices. We strolled down a hallway, where four original works from Norman Rockwell hung. They were oil paintings of people who were visiting the White House. The collection is known as, "So, You're Here to See the President"—priceless works of art. I grew up loving Norman Rockwell, so I was overwhelmed. The hallway led us to the Press Briefing Room. I imagined our current president standing at the podium, answering questions with his polite manner that only he could deliver. No matter the president or press secretary, when they left the room, someone was going to be disappointed.

"Might be you someday," I said to Nora. She faced away from the podium, like she had been there countless times before.

"They say that press secretary is a thankless job," she said.

The group began to move out of the room and down the hall. Through the chatter, I poked her shoulder. "Who said I was talking about press secretary?"

Nora's eyelids softened, and she gazed at me without saying a word. I enjoyed paying a compliment to a lady, just at the right time and setting. I hoped that it struck a chord with her. But beyond my own selfish reasons, I thought she might like to know that in this unforgiving town, she still had one admirer.

Next was the Cabinet Room, where the table must have been built based on its size. It was hard not to imagine a full house of people hanging on the president's every word. Maybe he would take a break and walk the dog in the Rose Garden. This was not a figment of my imagination, I was really in the White House.

Two gentlemen opened the door to the Oval Office, and I thought I might faint.

"Take a seat, son," Mr. Gibson said as we walked inside.

Standing frozen in my wing tips with sweaty palms, I decided that I'd seen all I needed to see. Whatever favors Mr. Gibson needed, I would not let him down. Endless possibilities ran through my head.

We sat for pictures on the couches adjacent to the president's famed *Resolute Desk*, which had been made from timbers of a British naval ship and given as a gift by Queen Victoria. Mr. Gibson seemed in his element. He sat on one of the couches with Mr. Lynch and chatted loud enough for me to hear: "We agreed on everything right here in this room. Then we took a walk out to the Rose Garden and posed for pictures. Mr. Yoshida just ate it up."

"That really changes everything," Mr. Lynch said. He leaned closer to Mr. Gibson. "And who made the arrangements?"

Mr. Gibson stood up, placed his hand on Mr. Lynch's shoulder. "You're looking at him."

They both laughed.

I wanted so badly to know what they were talking about, but I was in no place to ask. I continued to stroll around the office as the other guests posed for pictures. A few things caught my eye: the bronze *Bronco Buster* sculpture from 1895, symbolizing Theodore Roosevelt's famed Rough Riders; a bust of Abraham Lincoln, and the oil painting of President George Washington over the mantel. As I stood and stared in wonder, Nora approached my side. She didn't say anything, she just looked on as if we were in a museum. I suppose we were.

I looked toward Mr. Gibson. "What do you suppose they're talking about?"

"Who knows with him," Nora said. "Either world peace or world war. Whichever he can profit from the most."

"You've got the South in your mouth. Where did you grow up?"

"Virginia. Outside of Richmond. Why?" She looked at me with a squint in her eyes, like I was intruding.

"Just curious is all."

I enjoyed watching Mr. Gibson. I'd seen him as a loose cannon in other environments, but when he needed to perform, to shine, to lobby—he was good. Aside from the showing off, and the snubbing of valets and waiters, his apparent love for erotic photography and lord knows what else still weighed fresh in my mind. I didn't know if I could trust him. For all I knew, I might have linked myself to a sex cult, where I'd experience sexual pleasure in a way people only dreamed about—sex without limits. *I might have.* As I glanced over at Nora, a feeling of euphoria came over me, and I needed to walk it off.

As we got up to leave, I looked closely at the oil painting of President Lincoln. "The best president ever?" Len Tabott, the nightly news anchor asked me as he gazed at the painting. He was that guy with the face for television: perfect posture, thick hair, and an endearing voice. He and I were opposites, and I wondered if he might be a threat to Nora.

"Hard to argue."

"Indeed," he said. "So, West Point, I hear."

His inquiry caught me off guard, and I tried not to act startled. "I'll try like hell. Standing here, anything seems possible." *Mr. Gibson must be telling these people that I'm a future cadet. If only.*

I ambled over to the Resolute Desk and ran my hand along its smooth surface. I couldn't help but think about President Kennedy. We've never had a president that didn't take the job serious, but JFK, if he had any faults, it was from far too much ambition I guess. What a terrible thing to witness back then.

"Go ahead," Mr. Gibson said.

I woke from my trance. "Sir?"

"Take a seat. You'll never get this opportunity again," he said. "Well," he got the attention of a few guests, "at least not anytime soon." His remark drew lots of laughs.

I just stared at the desk. Most everyone was engaged in conversation, including Nora. I took a long breath and walked across the presidential rug to the desk near the opposite side and looked out the window. I stood behind the desk and pulled out the leather chair. The feeling of sinking into the president's black leather chair was instantly imbedded in my memory. I held the scene in my mind, trying to memorize it, trying to envision Norman Rockwell himself painting it for me. And in another flash of selfishness, I thought about what it would feel like to wake up to Nora and our kids, have breakfast on a Saturday, and report to the people's office to tighten up some loose ends, maybe call the defense secretary for nine holes at Burning Tree. It was a moment I'll never forget.

Mr. Gibson looked at me with boredom, like I should've kicked my feet up or something.

"Man," was all I said.

A sudden flash caught my eye from across the room. I got startled and jumped to my feet. It was Nora. Apparently, she was carrying a camera in her purse and snapped the photo just in the nick of time. I mouthed the word "No" to her. She gave me a grin and a playful wink, making me want to chase her to the Lincoln Bedroom.

Everyone laughed. Except me. I could just see myself trying to explain this to my Aunt Emma and Uncle Jack.

The group began to get up and follow our tour guide out. Our evening seemed to be wrapping up. As the party moved from the office, Nora pulled me back and pushed me into a wicker chair that sat right next to the door. I looked up at her in astonishment, not understanding what she was doing. After looking outside, she then sat on my lap and got her camera out again. She turned the lens to face us and began snapping random pictures.

What is this woman doing?

With a kiss on my neck, she took another picture. She grabbed my tie and led me back to the Resolute Desk, this time for a more proper photo—not as steamy. I couldn't say no.

She hurried out of the Oval Office, and I followed. She was halfway down the hall when I reached the first turn. I took chase and could hear her laughing. At the stairwell just past the Cabinet Room, I got hold of her by the waist. She turned back, and her smile took on a look of desire. It was the first time I sensed that she might have had feelings for me, and I couldn't contain myself. Just as I was about to move in on her, we heard our group. Her tight hips in my hands, Nora pulled free and led me down the stairs.

She looked like *the* American girl. If she weren't taken, she had to be one of the most eligible bachelorettes in the city.

"You act like you've been here before," I said.

She glanced at me, looked ahead, and straightened her face. "That's how we're all supposed to be acting, Calvin." Nora's elegant voice resembled the sound of a sword being drawn from a sheath. She wasn't just all fun and games.

We joined the group on the ground floor and had a peek into the Situation Room. Mr. Gibson walked in and leaned on one of the brown leather chairs. "The Woodshed," he said. "Some of the most important decisions in the world are made right here." I listened intently. I pictured all the seats filled with people making decisions about the lives of Americans. I thought of my aunt and uncle, of my mom and grandma. *Politics is a noble profession*, my Uncle Jack once said—and I gained a new veneration for it that day.

The Ambassador of Romania, James Sheppard, spoke up, "But often a hasty call to arms." There was a further exchange, but I was out of earshot. Nora had most of my attention. She and I walked across the hall to the Navy Mess. She flung back her flowing brown hair and walked with confidence in front of me.

A bottle of Krug champagne was chilling in a silver ice bucket when we entered the room. "The proper etiquette is to wait for everyone else," Nora said. I looked at my watch and began to whistle. The room had walls of rustic wood, reminiscent of an admiral's quarters. Rightly so, since the U.S. Navy ran the room, including the food. There were round white-clothed tables with navy blue leather chairs and large framed paintings of naval ships at sea.

A server in a white jacket arrived with a large tray perched on his shoulder. Being that we were the only group there and that it was well after midnight, it was plain to see that he'd been waiting for us. The tray contained shrimp cocktail, smoked salmon on cucumber slices, and bread and butter; the butter having the presidential seal imprinted on it, naturally. For dessert, there was a cart with fresh fruit on small pastries and jelly beans. Mr. Gibson shook his head at me, which I interpreted as no booze. However, once the waiter and tour guide left us, he brought me a glass of bubbly. "Son, I'm pleased that you joined us tonight. It shows commitment."

"Thank you, sir. I'm grateful for the opportunity."

He stepped back and tapped his glass with a butter knife. "To good friends and a memorable evening. Hail to the Chief!"

45

Chapter Six

"When I was your age," my uncle said, "I was studying Latin."

I had stopped by his home the following Saturday morning to do a few chores. My aunt and uncle lived in a modest Cape Cod on Honesty Way, just blocks from Whitman. It was mere days after my visit to the White House, and I was still euphoric with that brand-new-day feeling. I wanted to talk about it with him, but that would ruin everything for me. If he or my mom found out I was on a midnight tour of the White House with my lobbyist friend who the family barely knew, the party would be over. And being that Nora instructed me not to share anything, it just wasn't an option. Keeping it a secret was killing me. I had to tell someone.

"I don't think you can take Latin at Whitman," I said.

"I took it in a one room schoolhouse. Calvin, do you know what the Monroe Doctrine is?" He put down the *Washington Post* and looked over his glasses at me. He was seated in his usual brown leather Barcalounger in the kitchen. My Aunt Emma was back in Charleston, South Carolina, for a child literacy conference, so it was just the two of us.

Anxiety set in because, for one, I didn't know about the Monroe Doctrine, and two, at that moment, I didn't really care. I was much more interested in the Secret Service, limousines, swanky parties, and Nora. I still hadn't figured out what I had fallen into since wrecking Mr. Gibson's car, but whatever it was, it gave me chills up my spine, and I loved it. I wanted in. I yearned to be part of Mr. Gibson's group, and I was willing to do whatever it took to play a role.

"I haven't learned about that yet." I said.

"I don't know what they're teaching you kids these days, but you need to be studying history, language, different cultures, and the humanities. I'm sure your mom would agree."

Jack Gregory, my great-uncle, was serving his fourth term as the Democratic senator from South Carolina and had at one time been considered by his party to run for the Oval Office. He was in his late sixties, was a Marine Corps veteran, and still chopped his own firewood. He would come unglued if he knew where I had been earlier that week. It was one thing to visit the White House with the public and see the Blue and Red Rooms in the afternoon, it's another when you're stumbling out of a limo into the West Wing at midnight, eating shrimp and sipping champagne like you own the place. I figured he would find out about Mr. Gibson sooner or later, but as far as he would know, I caddied for him—that was it. He went back to the paper.

"Mom's a little hot with me today," I said. His eyebrows perked up above his glasses, which sat snug upon his sharp, hawkish nose.

"For what reason?"

"Got home late from work the other night, and not paying enough attention to school."

"Calvin, your schoolwork should be your number-one priority. Don't take her disappointment lightly."

"I know. But there's other stuff out there besides school right now."

"Like?"

Like Nora. "I don't know. It's a big, beautiful world out there, anything can happen."

"Well, that's just silly," he said with his long Southern drawl. "And if you want to play any part in it, you've got to do well in school. Are you working too much at that golf club?"

"No, sir." I thought about Mr. Gibson. "You know, I had the pleasure of caddying for a guy one afternoon. Everybody treated him like a star. Turns out he's my grandma's neighbor."

"Who was that?"

"Mr. Eli Gibson."

My uncle got up out of his chair. "Son, there are people that represent everything that's wrong in this town, and he's one of them. You need to avoid people like that at all costs. Do you understand me?"

The last thing I wanted to do was anger a member of the Senate, let alone my uncle. But in the back of my mind, I knew my hunch was right. Something was scandalous about Mr. Gibson, and now I just had to know what it was.

"Yes, sir. I understand. It kind of happened on accident."

"I don't give a coon's ass how it happened. You are to stay away from men like Mr. Gibson." His eyes narrowed something fierce. "Are we clear?"

"Yes, sir. Oh, and Mom wanted to invite you and Aunt Emma to dinner next week for my birthday."

"Birthday, eh?"

"It's a big one," I said. "I finally get to vote."

He grinned.

***

I got home and immediately went to the third floor via the service elevator, and sure as hell, the door to Mr. Gibson's place was open.

I could hear his voice; he was directing someone. I decided to gently knock. The room fell silent. I could smell the cigar smoke and his fancy cologne. I knocked again. This time I heard him coming to the door. I didn't feel nervous. I felt calm, like visiting family or something. I was part of the pack now.

The door flung open, "Well, hello, chap," Mr. Gibson said.

"Hope I'm not intruding."

Mr. Gibson gave me a long, squinty-eyed stare and invited me in. I felt uneasy because he looked a little weathered, like he'd overserved himself, and there was another person in the room: a tall, muscular guy in a dark suit and a red-striped tie.

"Tell me your name again, son," Mr. Gibson said.

"Calvin Ducane."

"Calvin, right…Calvin, this is Phillip, one of my colleagues."

I walked toward the guy and went in for a strong handshake, but his was a bit on the soft side. It wasn't any cause for concern, it just seemed odd to me considering his size. So, I did what my Uncle Jack had trained me to do: I looked him in the eye and repeated his name. "Phillip, Calvin Ducane, nice meeting you."

I'm not sure if my Uncle Jack's take on meeting people is the best, but I always enjoyed watching him work a room. He had an aura of confidence about him that was incredibly genuine. Part of it was he wanted to see how trustworthy you were by looking you in the eye, two, he wanted to see how you would react to his distinct voice; and three, he wanted to check the firmness of your grip and if you truly were *happy to meet him*.

This guy Phillip didn't seem so happy to meet me. He could've had it either way. It seemed like he was getting ready to leave anyway, so no harm, no foul. His shirt was a touch too tight, and his head bulged. He had a large jaw and resembled a football player, like he was a tight end somewhere years back. He was about six-four and not much for personality. We did the normal exchanges, and he left, closing the door all the way. I was waiting to see Mr. Gibson get up and prop the door open, but he didn't.

I had a thing for making myself at home; I got that from my grandma. She did it in an almost rude fashion, so if I could break that habit, I'd be forever grateful. I liked to open people's refrigerators, look at pictures on the mantel, and grab books off shelves, lots of weird things like that. It was a little tacky, but I'm fascinated by people, and I want to know their stories.

"Where is this from?"

"Don't touch that, it's priceless. It's from Argentina." It was a small carving of some sort. *It doesn't look priceless*. I put it back.

"What about the vase?"

"It's a gift from the Mayor of Tokyo, 1979."

We went around the room, me picking things up, him nervously telling me where they were from.

I picked up a large glass piece. "One of those decanter things, like from the Dolley Madison."

"Very good. But that one is *Moser*, from Prague."

His responses were like I was somewhat bothering him by asking, but I think he also enjoyed showing off. I wandered into the office, and there were

51

a few pictures framed and sitting on the glass shelving of his wet bar, which he had obviously frequented tonight. I looked at one picture of him and about seven other men, all in tuxedos and sitting in a circle on a patio somewhere. One of those men was Ronald Reagan. I looked closer and saw two Asian-looking men; they were both smiling—no doubt proud to be seated in the company of the president of the United States. I thought about our White House tour and remembered Mr. Gibson talking about this photo—it was the Rose Garden.

As far as I was concerned, Ronald Reagan might as well have been seated right there in the office. His days as president were quickly dwindling, and the election campaigns were in their final month. For a moment, I wondered how close I would get to the president, to the power players. It was a manic feeling. Maybe it had something to do with my rebellion, but wherever it originated, I liked it.

I asked Mr. Gibson about the picture, but all I got was, "Yeah, you like that? The Rose Garden." That was all he said. I suppose it spoke for itself. The last photo on the bottom shelf was of the young man that could pass for my twin. It was time to ask about it.

"And who is this?"

"Oliver. My son."

"No kidding? That's cool."

"Yeah, that's in the French Riviera last year."

"Monte Carlo?"

"Close to there. Saint Jean-Cap-Ferrat. I'll be going there soon. You should come along."

"To Europe? Yeah, wouldn't that be nice. I'm hoping that the Army sends me over there, but we'll see."

"Well, like I told you, you should be focusing on your future career...and going to that public school isn't going to help you. You should be going to Langdon." He paused. "I can make that happen."

His words, or I should say, his tone spooked me. He walked back behind his desk. "You stick with me, son, I'll make you a millionaire." He lit a fresh cigar and leaned back in his leather chair. From this point forward, no matter what this guy was involved in, I was all in. Unlike most kids who were either related to or connected to people in Washington, I had no interest in doing this cookie-cutter lifestyle. I wanted excitement and danger, and I wanted it right then and there. And something told me sticking with Mr. Gibson would give me all the excitement I could handle.

Chapter Seven

Mr. Gibson created his wealth and influence by mocking a former Washington socialite named Perle Mesta. Perle had considerable wealth, was a Washington socialite during the Truman administration, and was considered *the* most powerful hostess in the city during those years. She threw lavish parties, and being on her guest list meant that you had made it in Washington. When asked how one might make a name for themselves in the capital, her response was, "Hang a lamb chop in the window." I remembered Mr. Gibson saying that to me when we had first met. I remember feeling awestruck, like it was a line from a scary movie.

Of course, all this entertaining was essentially part of a social Ponzi scheme. Washington goes through an enormous transition of power every four years, which displaces people of considerable intellect and status. This makes a great stage for those trying to rebuild themselves, much like a Jay Gatsby. So, for all Perle's effort and influence, President Truman appointed her as the Ambassador to Luxembourg. Membership does have its privileges.

I had a hunch that Mr. Gibson wanted to emulate Perle Mesta. Especially since whenever he threw one of his opulent dinners, or even went out for dinner, it was always lamb chops and expensive wines. Mr. Gibson had somehow climbed the Washington social ladder to where he was now dining with names such as journalists William Safire and Ted Koppel, former CIA Director William Casey, and Marine Corps Commandant Alfred M. Gray. These are but a few of the names to have crossed paths with Mr. Gibson. I had a chance to meet several of them, but at the time, I didn't know who they were, except for Ted Koppel of course. Mr. Gibson was "running with the big dogs," as my uncle used to say. Certainly, it was all legit, and he had been in D.C. since '79, so by now, he no longer had to "hang a lamb chop in the window."

After the conversation I had with Mr. Gibson about Langdon Prep School, I decided to share some of it with my mom. Whenever I brought up Mr. Gibson's name, she had little to say. However, she had asked a while back about why I was so intrigued with him, and I never responded. It was a fair question. As much as the free gin and tonics were a perk, when I saw the fleet of limos, Audis, and sports cars, I knew something exciting was about to happen. I couldn't tell her though, and I wasn't going to share the whole "make you a millionaire" conversation.

"He's a very bright man. I can see him as a mentor, I guess."

"You met him where? Parking his car?"

"Yes, and I caddied for him. We had a great conversation."

"Well, there's a surprise…you, striking up conversations again. It's great that you're so outgoing and that you like people, but we're not in Ohio anymore. You've got to be careful about who you're interacting with. I'm not so sure about this guy."

"I'm just enjoying getting to know the neighbors."

"That's fine, but…did he tell you what he does for a living?"

"He's a lobbyist of some sort. He's done work in Vietnam, Japan. And there was a picture of him and Ronald Reagan on his mantel." That picture of him sitting with Reagan really threw me for a loop. I was so impressed.

"I worked for Ronald Reagan…couldn't stand him," my grandma said. She loved to talk about important people, especially presidents.

It was cool to me that my grandma had headed up the Export-Import Bank, but you'd never know she was retired by having a conversation with her. She had worked under four presidents and had been instrumental in the success of Exim Bank. She was seated at the head of the table, wearing her yellow apron and taking in our conversation. My grandma liked the idea of me befriending the neighbors, especially one that was a Washington socialite. Having Reagan in common, if Mr. Gibson ever stepped foot in her condo, she'd never let him leave.

She couldn't wait to meet him, and her wish came true that very night. Right as we were finishing up dinner, the doorbell rang. I got up to answer it, and my grandma, of course, was right behind me. I opened the door, and standing in front of me was Mr. Gibson, his employee Phillip, and another big, tall man who could've passed for Phillip's brother. Mr. Gibson stepped inside, and the other two men stood there, awkward as hell, holding what appeared to be a pastry box. I didn't need to introduce anyone because Mr. Gibson was already standing close to my grandma, talking and laughing with great enthusiasm. He took the box out of Phillip's hands and composed himself, looking for everyone's attention. He was obviously intoxicated.

"Grandmama, I've heard so much about you. I understand you've recently retired from XM Bank. I decided to recognize you for your service with a sweet surprise."

"What is it?" my grandma said. She looked at both my mom and I as if to make sure we were as eager as she was.

Mr. Gibson opened the box, and inside was a small, round cake covered with yellow frosting.

"Look here, your name is Maggie, right?"

"Why, yes," my grandma said, peering down into the box.

He read the cake's lettering to her. "To Grandmama, with much affection."

"Oh, look! Linda, come look at what Mr.….Mr.….?"

"Gibson. Eli Gibson. I'm happy to finally meet you both."

My mom coldly shook hands with Mr. Gibson and then backed away. The two men still stood at the door, looking like bouncers at a night club, and my grandma basically groped Mr. Gibson, whose lips were a shade of purple from too much wine. And I lingered in the background, acting like this was all okay.

As the two of them flattered each other, my mom went back to the dining room and began clearing dinner dishes. My grandma and Mr. Gibson had made their way into the living room, where they looked over a framed document from the bank, commemorating my grandma's service for the last sixteen years.

"I liked Jimmy Carter, he was a fine man, and then I worked under Ronald Reagan." She rolled her eyes, giving away that she was a Democrat. Mr. Gibson, clearly a Republican, didn't seem to care.

"Oh, look at your lovely patio," he said. "Can you show it to me?"

"Please!" my grandma said. "I just had it redone last year, and I love my garden."

I didn't want to leave the two of them alone, plus I wanted to hear their conversation. As my grandma pointed out the different plants she'd been growing and how the small, stone fountain had been installed, Mr. Gibson crossed his arms and politely listened. He seemed to hurry her along, but it wasn't rude by any means.

"I take it heading up XM Bank sent you many places," he said.

"I've been to seventy-five different countries, if you can believe it." She raised her head slightly and looked for approval. "No more airports for this gal. I don't mind not being so busy anymore."

Mr. Gibson went on to tell her about places he'd visited as a journalist and a lobbyist. They were getting along handsomely. I appreciated him not trying to one-up my grandma. He was cool in his approach, and it further interested me in continuing our agreement.

He paused and leaned into her slightly. "I'll bet your brother is pretty busy."

"Who, Jack? Oh, he works round the clock. I didn't know you'd met him." I was taken aback. I never said a word about my uncle to him. I made a point not to. *How did he know?* He never answered her.

The night winded down quickly, just the usual hum of scattered traffic down on Mass Avenue remained. Mr. Gibson and his Roman wrestlers were beginning to leave when I caught him at the door and discreetly said, "Mr. Gibson, I never told you I was related to Jack Gregory."

"No?" he said. "Must have heard it elsewhere." He gave my grandma a hug goodbye and looked over her shoulder at me and winked. Then, he left.

"Well, that sure was interesting," my mom said.

"He was very gracious…and this cake is wonderful!" my grandma said, with a mouthful.

"I don't know," my mom said. "This whole thing is weird."

"Mom, he's harmless. Those guys work for him, and he lobbies downtown. Besides, he's going to help me investigate schools. He's connected. He promised."

"Grandmama? What the hell was that all about?"

"He's terrific!" my grandma said.

My mom just closed her eyes briefly, shook her head, and walked upstairs.

Chapter Eight

On a few occasions, I had the opportunity to watch my Uncle Jack speak on the Senate floor. He had a folksy manner that came naturally, having grown up in the South, and he had learned this at a young age when a teacher paid him a wonderful compliment. He had been asked to read aloud to the class, and upon finishing the passage, the teacher said, "Doesn't he have a wonderful voice, class? Doesn't he read beautifully? Wouldn't it be a shame if Jack didn't use his God-given gift for speaking? Surely, he could make something of himself because he speaks and reads so beautifully."

He told that story as a small-town lawyer, as a governor, as a Senator, as an uncle, in grocery stores, and to any passerby. I was sick of hearing that goddamned story, but it stayed with me, and I always try to emulate my Uncle Jack.

I think those experiences led me to enroll in debate class at Whitman. I really did want to be like him, but I was also blessed with the gift of gab, and I figured I could nail the class.

The classroom itself was on the far west end of the building, where the sun nestled in during the afternoon. The room had a yellowish tint and was often warm because of that westerly sun. The teacher, Mr.

Powell, was a calm, good-natured guy, and he loved what he did for a living—teaching young people how to argue, or argue constructively, I should say.

Mr. P, as we called him, had dark, uncombed hair to go along with his mid-sized potbelly and a slight redness to his skin, which told me he liked to tip a few back in his leisure time. But he was my favorite teacher, and I wanted to do well in his class.

Meeting Mr. Gibson and staying up most of the night had me exhausted. And by the time I ate something for lunch and walked into the warm, yellow room filled with sunshine, my exhaustion felt like some type of tranquilizer.

Mr. Powell was the last person I wanted to disappoint at Whitman, but unfortunately, I did. One afternoon, after being awake most of the previous night, I fell asleep in his debate class and remained asleep until long after the class had ended, until it was just Mr. Powell and I left in the room. When I woke up, he was sitting across from me, staring.

"Oh man, I'm so sorry, Mr. P." I wiped the drool from my cheek. "I haven't been sleeping."

"It appears that way, Calvin. Is everything all right?"

He asked it out of concern, like the boy asleep in his room was some sort of transient orphan who needed a hunk of bread and a pair of shoes.

"This had nothing to do with boredom, Mr. P. I love this class. Just haven't been sleeping." He packed up his briefcase, and I followed him out of the classroom and down the wide hallway bright with fluorescent lighting.

"Calvin, if you simply apply yourself, you could be a strong candidate for our debate team next spring."

"You think so?"

"I do. The question is, do *you*?"

He was looking at me like a father might look at his son, as though he wanted his kid to believe in himself. For some reason, it was a bit unnerving because I had grandiose thoughts of distinguishing myself in the military, getting into politics, running for office, and proving to all the doubters that I would be the voice of a generation.

My Uncle Charles, my mom's brother, once told me, "If you don't get focused and start doing something constructive with yourself, you'll wind up living amongst the dregs of society." Those words would haunt me, *the dregs of society*. I needed to flourish, and I had to do it fast to prove to people like my uncles that I'm not a dreg, even if I had to spend time amongst those dregs to get my life going, to learn those valuable lessons, to earn the rite of passage. The dregs of society were people too. Standing there, lost in thought, I watched the other students walk past on their way to their next classes. But one of them didn't fit in. One of them, a female with straight dark hair, wearing a navy blazer and tan skirt was looking in our direction from across the hall.

Nora.

"Well, give it some thought," Mr. Powell said. "In a couple of weeks, we'll be having a Lincoln-Douglas debate. You'll learn the topic a few days beforehand. I think you'll do well if you prepare yourself. In the meantime, get some sleep."

"I will. Thanks, Mr. P."

I waited for him to move along before I walked toward Nora. "Follow me," I said. There was no need for me to be nervous, but I was. *What is she doing here?* We walked outside toward the dome that covered the gymnasium. The sun was bright and made me squint. She put on a pair of Coach sunglasses, which made her look scandalous.

"Little late for lunch," I said.

Nora showed no reaction. "Eli needs you to make a run."

"I should be done in—"

"It's urgent." She began walking toward the parking lot as if I were to follow.

"Kind of risky for me to take off right now. Come back next week when I'm eighteen, and I can sign myself out. But not today."

Nora pulled her keys out of her brown Louis Vuitton handbag. "We'll take care of that." I thought of Gibson putting her up to this because he knew I wouldn't say no. She was my weakness.

About twenty minutes later, we were in the Audi, idling outside a massive, modern-looking home on Arizona Avenue. It was three stories of stucco and stone, hardly any windows in the front. "It's in the back," she said. She stared straight ahead, like she was ready to get this over with. I looked in the back seat and discovered a package wrapped in brown paper and secured with ample Scotch tape.

"What is it?"

"Not your concern. You're just the delivery boy."

Grabbing the package, I slipped out of my seatbelt and walked quickly up to the front gate, where I found an intercom with a small white button, like the one at the Foxhall's back entrance.

I rang the buzzer. *Nothing.* I rang it again. And again. I turned around and looked at Nora, who wasn't paying attention to me. Finally, a female voice that sounded foreign, perhaps from the islands somewhere, came over the speaker: "Help you?"

"Good afternoon. I have a delivery from Mr. Eli Gibson." More silence. The gate unlocked. I opened it up and walked to the front door, where a housekeeper in a gray and white uniform waited. She didn't look happy to see me.

I handed her the package. She looked at it and then glanced back at me. "Gibson?"

"Yes, ma'am."

She slowly shut the door, staring at me the entire time as if worried about sudden movements. I heard the deadbolt slam.

"Have a good day." I walked off some of my nervous energy on the way back to the car.

"Who answered?" Nora said.

"Housekeeper."

"Some house, isn't it?"

"Like it's from the future." It really did appear that way. It was more of a compound than anything. I wanted to ask who owned it and many other questions, but that was not part of the deal.

"What was it you said about signing yourself out of school soon?" Nora said.

"Something I found out from a friend recently. Once you turn eighteen you can sign out of school based on the Age of Majority law. Not that I'm looking for excuses to skip school, but it'll be nice considering."

"Considering?"

"Considering I'll need some flexibility, especially with the election and inauguration coming up."

"And in case you want to get married or run for office," she said.

"There's also that, I suppose." She drove down toward Connecticut Avenue and made a left-hand turn. I smiled and looked at her. "My own legal guardian, free to do whatever I please."

"Careful what you wish for, Calvin."

Chapter Nine

"Congratulations on winning tonight, Uncle Jack," I said.

"Why thank you, Calvin. And happy birthday. Did you register to vote yet?" All the ladies at the table laughed.

"I would've had to skip school," I said. "Maybe tomorrow if I can get there before they close." We were seated in a large leather booth at Houston's in Georgetown. The restaurant was relatively dark besides the hanging lamps that shined down on the tables. I had turned eighteen the day before, and we had decided to celebrate after my uncle competed in a debate against the Republican senator from Iowa. It was probably the first time in a while that I could take my mind off my obligations to Mr. Gibson. Watching my uncle on stage, casually leaning against the podium and schooling the entire room made me immensely proud.

After all the ladies ordered, I handed my menu to the waiter. "I'll have the stuffed shrimp and a Caesar salad."

"Look," my uncle said. "Calvin's got class." His compliment confused me, so I just smiled. I suppose it was because I didn't order the porterhouse, and he was footing the bill.

"Of course, he does, look who raised him," my Aunt Emma said.

There were seven of us at the table, and we all seemed to be talking at once over bread and butter.

"Calvin, I'm sure I shared this story with your mother once or twice, but I don't think you've had the pleasure of hearing it," my Uncle Jack said. "Growing up in Darlington, our porch wrapped around the house and looked out over a meadow. Our dog's name was *Babe*, and in her younger years, she loved to chase anything that moved." My sister Sam smiled, and her eyes lit up at him and his dog sitting on the porch together in the sweltering South Carolina heat. "On one occasion, a marsh rabbit sauntered into the yard and caught old Babe's attention. Now, Babe had just woken from a nap, but she still went barreling off the porch, barking like mad and the chase was on."

Two waiters came and delivered our dinners and filled our water glasses. Uncle Jack waited for them to leave before he continued. "It didn't take long before the other dogs that lived close by took notice, and they all joined in, following Babe across the creek and up the meadow. But then a funny thing happened. Just as the rabbit reached the crest of the horizon, the pack of dogs all turned back and gave up the chase…all but old Babe. She stayed in hot pursuit. Now, why do you suppose that was, Calvin?"

I knew this was coming but was still caught off guard. My mind remained on the porch of his childhood home. "It was supper time," I said.

He was holding a large steak knife and about to carve into a pork chop when he waved it toward me, the blade shining in the light. "Actually, that's not a bad answer," he said, and we all laughed. "But no, the reason was because the other dogs lost sight of the rabbit once he hit the crest. And if you lose sight of it, you will lack the passion and will to keep up the chase." His steak knife scraped his plate. He paused and looked at me closely. "Keep your eye on that rabbit, son. Now, pass me the salt and pepper."

Everyone dove right into their dinners and talked about the debate and how well my Uncle Jack had done. It felt surreal to be seated at that table. After all I'd been through in my youth, living in a Rust Belt town, all the trouble, almost failing out of school. And now I'm sitting with the senator receiving my favorite birthday gift—wisdom. What he told me that night made me stop and think about my current agenda. I had a lot on my plate. Some of it was more than I had bargained for, but I couldn't bring myself to walk away. And if anyone at that table knew, I'd probably be on the first bus back to Cleveland. There was only one problem with what I'd learned from Uncle Jack that night—even though it was great advice, I was more than likely going to apply it to my employment with Mr. Gibson.

We ended dinner with our server bringing out an entire New York-style cheesecake, with strawberries and candles and all. I opened some cards and read all the notes. My family is big on greeting cards and writing something affectionate in them. Although I enjoyed the evening, for some reason, I felt alone. I thought about my dad and my other siblings. Things were different now, and I was adapting too quickly. I was starting a whole new life. Starting all over.

"Calvin, what's fifteen percent of a hundred and twenty bucks?" my uncle said.

I accepted the challenge of him quizzing me and thought for a moment. Like I didn't get enough of that from my mom. I was stuck for a second. *If ten percent of a hundred twenty is twelve bucks, then,* "About eighteen bucks."

"Give or take?"

"No. No, it's definitely eighteen bucks." I couldn't help but wonder what Mr. Gibson would tip on the same tab. *Probably fifty bucks.*

Chapter Ten

Mr. Gibson drove up the hill to the Foxhall, the headlamps of the Mercedes glowing up the driveway. I couldn't figure out why he went back and forth between his home in Kalorama and the condominium. He had told me that the condo was for his out-of-town guests, and I had seen my share of those. It usually consisted of some suit whisking off a young, scantily clad woman—or sometimes a young man. I stopped up to say hello. Mr. Gibson was walking back from his office into the living room.

"Why do you always leave the door open?" I said.

"Let my friends know I'm home." He was dressed casually in a dark cashmere jacket and slacks along with a blue button-down shirt. I wanted to dress like that someday. Mr. Gibson glanced in the room-length mirror, ran his hands through his thin, brown hair, and adjusted his jacket. Whatever he was getting into that night, it would probably go into the wee hours.

"So, when can I start?' I said. I received a stern look from him. My stomach dropped. I must've asked a forbidden question or something. As much as Mr. Gibson intrigued me, he displayed enough wild behavior for me not to trust him. He looked out over

Massachusetts Avenue, watching the traffic. Living up on the hill at the Foxhall made for a spectacular view, especially at night.

"You've already started, son. You've fulfilled your first assignment. Now it's time to get acclimated. And do you know how to get acclimated quickly?"

"How's that?"

"Don't ask fucking questions."

"I'm sor—"

"And don't be fucking sorry."

He walked into the office and began pouring a drink. I decided that I wanted to get out of there, so I chose not a have one, even if he offered.

"You'll be taking orders, plain and simple," he said. "Nora or I will give you the specifics. You carry them out in a timely, accurate manner, and I pay you in cash upon completion. You're now the courier for the organization. Do you understand?"

"Without a doubt." I understood, just not sure I agreed.

"Some of my work is conducted, how should I say, out of the public eye. It's paramount that you keep your duties to yourself."

"Okay."

"And lastly, for today anyway," he tossed a set of keys to me, "you need to learn your way around the city. Get yourself a map, fill up the tank." He pulled a wad of cash from his jacket pocket and flipped me a hundred-dollar bill. "And get familiar with Capitol Hill, the airport, and the Northwest neighborhoods. The Supra will be your work vehicle, unless I need it for something."

My mind spun with possibilities. I envisioned myself cruising around the city with Nora and her unshakable confidence, with her eventually falling for whatever charm I believed I had. It was unlikely, but a goal nonetheless. I decided to get out of there before he changed his mind.

"I'll make you proud," I said.

"You'd better."

***

The following morning was not my typical commute to school. I shook my head as I drove out of the Foxhall. I couldn't believe I had the Supra and that I was working for Mr. Gibson. This time I pulled into school with a car that fit in much better—no more Datsun pickup or my mom's Honda.

I turned right onto Bradley Boulevard, which intersected with my aunt and uncle's street, Honesty Way. There was a semi-steep incline to that stretch of road, which only lasted for a few seconds, but it was enough for me to lay on the throttle and zoom past their house, where I let out a loud, boyish scream. That was completely uncalled for, especially since I had just turned eighteen. However, Mr. Gibson had lent me a sports car, and I felt like showing off a little.

It was a gorgeous fall day, but warmer than I was used to. Early October in Ohio had a nip in the air that served as a forewarning: you'd better cherish these days because soon you'd be fighting the "gales of November" that blew in off the Great Lakes, often unannounced. If there were a season that I missed in Ohio, it was autumn. Sweatshirts, football, girls in tight jeans. I could still smell the leaf piles and black walnuts. As I made the turn onto Whittier, I became self-conscience. I had a feeling I would receive a few looks on campus, but I thought about what I was embarking on and decided that I was ready for anything.

In keeping with the kind of luck that I'd been having, Tom Blanchard, one of the football team captain, looked over the car and said, "Where's the truck?" It was just like him. Instead of saying *nice car*, he had to associate me with the Datsun. Little did he know that the Datsun belonged to a U.S. senator.

"I'm borrowing it from my boss."

"Who you working for?"

"Nobody you'd know."

Tom was a good six-foot-four and carried a temper. I didn't care though. I was too busy having fun in my clever new life on Embassy Row. I left him looking at the Supra and walked up to the school.

If there were ever a day that I wanted to practice my Age of Majority rights, this was it. With the golden sunlight of fall and the leaves beginning to turn, I thought about taking a spin into the city to learn my way around. Maybe some lunch, maybe drop by Nora's office, but it would have to wait. I had barely slept the night before, and the school day dragged.

I got a few more looks from people after school. By now, a couple friends that I hung out with in the library during study hall inquired about me and discovered some of my story, not like they had to pry or anything. I just wanted to blend in. My real ambitions weren't within the halls of that school—they were in a much larger theater, one that I had no business in. Of course, you couldn't tell me that.

Chapter Eleven

"How's it going at the country club?" My grandma asked with her usual enthusiasm. She had just returned from swimming at the Foxhall pool and wore her white terrycloth robe and light blue and yellow swim cap. Her raspy voice projected from the foyer of her condominium.

"So far, so good. Working a few times a week, but they'll need more of me soon. We sprint up and down three flights of stairs, so it's not easy." I glanced over at my mom, who was seated across from me at the dining room table, looking through a stack of folders.

"It's the right job for now," my mom said, "but you should shoot for twice a week. Your studies come first." She had that innate ability to make it sting when it had to. I didn't say anything. I just picked up my putter that was leaning against the sliding glass door and walked out onto the patio to putt a few balls across the green outdoor carpet. That's where I did most of my thinking—there and the rooftop.

I decided to pay another visit to Mr. Gibson. By now, we had exchanged numbers, but mostly I did the calling. I think he sensed that my mom didn't approve of anything that took me away from my studies. I was lying to her quite a bit, which was a shitty thing to do.

The least that I could do for her was to become a model citizen and create some wealth so that she wouldn't have to work anymore. That's what I was trying to do— only I thought I'd take a few shortcuts.

"What are you up to tonight?" my mom asked.

"Mr. Gibson is having a dinner party and invited me to stop up." This made my mom freeze in her tracks. I could see her cringe when she heard his name. She really found him to be rotten, but to me, he was harmless. Mostly anyway.

"You're going to dinner at Mr. Gibson's?" She asked this in a disappointed tone. I hated upsetting her, and it was worse when she showed it in her eyes. "You still have this fascination with him, I see."

"I'm just going for a little bit. I'm looking forward to meeting some of these people." It was a Friday night, so there wasn't any urgency to be home early. "I think a lot of them are on his staff."

"Just be careful."

"Careful?"

"Yes. Be careful."

"Look, I know you're concerned, but I'm lucky to know him. He has a hell of a lot more going on than anybody I know, that's for sure." I probably shouldn't have said that, but it came right out. "Outside of you, of course."

"What does this have to do with me?"

"It doesn't, that's my point. This guy might help me get into a good school or help me find an internship.

He's a mover and a shaker, a good guy to network with."

"When I told you about movers and shakers, he's not who I had in mind. Besides, that's for later in your life. Stop trying to grow up so fast." She knew that some things were a mess in my life, that's half the reason we moved to D.C. She also knew that I lashed out a lot because I questioned the way I'd been raised. Don't get me wrong, I was grateful, but I still owned a severe case of rebellion.

I wasn't a choirboy.

***

I knocked on Mr. Gibson's door, even though it was slightly open. Nobody seemed to notice, as there was quite a bit of noise coming from inside. I had put on some khakis and a sport coat, no tie, but a nice button-down shirt—typical Washington attire, so I was learning. It bothered me that my family made such an effort to make sure I had a nice appearance. That only mattered slightly back in Cleveland, but we were in Washington now, so we had to fit in. Things like that could bring out the rebel in me.

When I walked in, Mr. Gibson wasn't in the main living room. His dog, Winston, came running over to lick my hand and have me scratch his belly. As I kneeled, I got a good view of the scene. There was a semi-circle of guests, maybe eight people, all seated, visiting and cocktailing. One of them was Nora, who turned and noticed me walk in—she was in mid-laughter. I got a quick glance of her diamond earrings and her dark red nail polish. She seemed to be enjoying herself.

They were one hell of a distinguished group. One of them was a Marine Corps General with four stars; he had a razor-sharp haircut and a jaw like a hockey player. I recognized one from the national news, another from *Meet the Press*, and three more suits that looked like they belonged at a White House State Dinner. There were two caterers cooking in the kitchen; I could smell garlic, citrus, and fish being broiled. A male server in a tuxedo handed out hors d'oeuvres, a puff pastry and smoked salmon on toast points.

I wasn't at all uncomfortable, but I wondered where Mr. Gibson was. He finally came walking into the living room from the office. He looked to be beaming with pride to have all these bigwigs in his home. He poured a glass of white wine and handed it to me. These people had to know how young I was. On top of that, I felt he may have offered me the wine just a touch too graciously, almost like I was his date. Weird.

For such a classy gathering, he didn't seem to have the room for so many guests, and it turned out he had planned an entire dinner. Once the entrees arrived, everyone ate on couches, chairs, wherever they were seated during the cocktail hour. I sat in a wicker folding chair near the condo's foyer. There was a navy blue and white striped loveseat adjacent to me. I dove into the plate of white fish topped with crabmeat and a light sauce. It was served with some sort of rice and asparagus. It wasn't easy to eat from your lap. As I ate, I kept my eye on everybody.

One thing I discovered right off the rip was the group was all men again, except for Nora. Lucky for me, she was seated close. We shared the usual polite *hello, how are you*. She had her hair down that night, and the lamp behind me illuminated her gorgeous brown eyes. She had her legs crossed and her back arched as she ate her dinner.

"And what do you do besides go to school, Calvin?"

"Head of security. I do all the background checks at Foxhall."

She let out a slight giggle and covered her nose with her napkin. "I see. Have my results come back yet?"

"Yes, I'm afraid we're going to need some fingerprints." I was sneaking glances at her by this point. *Like your fingerprints on my back.*

Turns out Nora worked in public relations in the lobbying part of Washington, better known as *K Street*. When she spoke, the octave would drop a touch throughout the sentence and have just a hint of rasp. She was, in every sense of the word, a lady.

My mom had taught me you needed to have good manners with the opposite sex in social settings.

That included keeping your space, watching your eye contact, and, if you feel compelled to give a compliment, keep it modest.

I didn't feel the need to compliment Miss Nora; I believed there was a friendly connection over our few encounters. She was smart. She ran with the players. She was gorgeous. She was *a Washingtonian.* And she completely outclassed me.

We exchanged a few more words while eating, and I could tell she was tired of having the plate on her lap. I reached over to take it from her, and she seemed a bit startled. Once I had it in my hand, I took her silverware and linen and placed them on top of my own. There was a dark wooden end table between us, and I gently placed both of our plates on it. Nora smiled at my gesture and was on the border of blushing, but she didn't. She did exactly what I thought she would: she leaned slightly back on the couch, crossed her legs again and took a sip of wine.

"How do you like Gibson's group so far, Calvin?"

"Interesting bunch, I'd say. Once I finish up at Whitman, I'll be fully committed. Right now, I'm taking it all in. Growing up in Ohio, things have changed overnight for me." I got a nice smile from her over this. Mr. Gibson took notice of Nora and I hitting it off. He held court in the center of the room, throwing a tennis ball for Winston while his guests laughed along. It was starting to resemble a party. I pretended not to notice.

81

"I know what you mean. I grew up outside Richmond, moving here was a culture shock." She laughed a little at this. "I was also in high school when I moved here, so we have that in common." I caught her sneaking a peek at how I was dressed.

We sure do, you gorgeous, dark-haired goddess you.

Deep in my inflated ego, I felt a hunch that I was going to see Nora naked someday. The typical sex drive of a teenager, I suppose. It was always there, always lingering, disrupting my focus and making me crazy. All I could do was feed the beast.

After the guests and caterers had gone home, I hung around and had a few more splashes of wine. Nora was one of the last guests to leave. She, Mr. Gibson, and I had moved into his office, where he was showing off his pictures of Reagan, Ford, and others. There was a sword from Japan that he owned. I must admit, that thing was cool. With the sleek, strong design of its blade and unique character of the sash's decorations, I figured it to be worth a small fortune. I picked it up and studied it along with casual glances at my new crush. She was behind him looking at the pictures on his glass shelf above the bar. They had no doubt done this before. She was hanging on his arm, making me jealous. From where I was standing, I had a perfect view of Nora's curvy silhouette in the mirror across the room.

I was hoping she would pick up on me gazing at her, bold for an eighteen-year-old. When they got to the end of the shelf, where the pictures of Gibson and Reagan were, she glanced down to watch her step and looked right at me in the mirror. She gently tilted her head, flirted with a smile, and then brought her attention back to our host. I was spooked—Nora Dalton had just cast a spell on me. She excused herself to the restroom, and I stood up and moved toward Mr. Gibson. The wine had taken over, and I was trying to keep it together.

"She's awfully nice," I said.

"You like her, eh?" He was still admiring his collection of memorabilia. "Everyone likes Nora. She's come a long way, had her wings clipped early—you'll live a similar story, son. If you're lucky." I was taken aback by his statement. *This guy really has plans for me.*

A few moments had passed, and I was lost in my thoughts. Nora walked into the office. She immediately turned her attention to me.

"Well, the bell rings early, so I've got to say goodnight, Calvin."

"Yeah, I still have a security sweep to conduct." Her smile told me she enjoyed my corny humor.

"I'm sure I'll see you soon enough, but if you're ever down on the Hill, we should have lunch. I can show you around, introduce you to some people."

Jackpot.

"Movers and shakers? Count me in. Good night, Nora."

"Good night Calvin."

Mr. Gibson then escorted her to the main lobby, and I poured myself a nightcap.

Chapter Twelve

I took the service elevator home again, which had me feeling like a crafty burglar. As swanky as the Foxhall was, I really liked the bones of the place: the stairwells, the roof, and the grungy elevators.

My sister Samantha was still awake, watching some overly dramatic TV show, when I sneaked in. She had moved in with us temporarily after being between colleges. She was in her University of Colorado sweats and had her blonde hair pulled back in a ponytail. The sliding glass door was still open since it was quite warm for early October, and the night's traffic bustled down Mass Avenue.

"Were you at that Gibson guy's place again?" she said.

"Who wants to know?"

"You know, Mom thinks that dude's a creep." Mom had clearly put her up to this. She displayed the same enthusiasm she had for doing dishes or folding laundry. The sooner she lectured me, the sooner she could go to bed.

"Did Mom tell you to talk to me?"

"No…I'm just curious why you want to hang out with him." She barely looked at me. *Liar.*

"I'm not hanging out with him. He's basically grooming me to get into business with him someday, maybe sooner than later."

She burst into laughter and fell back into the couch.

"You think I'm joking? He said he'd make me a millionaire."

"Calvin," she started speaking serious now, as if she would slap me across the mouth if she could get away with it, "listen to yourself. That guy doesn't give two shits about you. You need to wake up and have a cup of reality. Something isn't right about that dude, and Mom and I are looking out for you. You need to talk to her, and do it soon before—"

"Before what? Before they kill me and hide the body? Whatever. I'm going up on the roof for a smoke. Come with me."

"Uh no, I'm going to bed." She clicked off the television. "Do yourself a favor, though, and talk to Mom before she pulls some drastic measures, okay?"

"Settle down, party police."

She looked back and gave me a sly squint. She didn't approve. No doubt my mom told her something or tipped her off enough for her to sit me down. And such was life living with three women. God forbid anybody had any fun around there.

***

The next morning, breakfast was quiet. It was the weekend, which meant hot sausage links and blueberry pancakes. It became a tradition in our family ever since my grandma starting growing blueberry bushes on the hill behind her home in Ohio. Cold milk, blueberry pancakes, sausage links, and fresh fruit. Always, always fresh fruit.

My grandma, in all her innocence, asked me, "How was the party?"

"It was nice. The fish was delicious. Grouper?"

"Oh, I love grouper. Did he have a nice crowd?" She looked at me with an almost jealous smile. That upset me a little. I didn't want her to think I was crowding in on her social life. She was in her seventies by then, and a lot of her free time was spent with her neighbors at the Foxhall.

"Yeah, maybe a dozen people, mostly conservatives. They talked a lot about the election. Uncle Jack and Aunt Emma wouldn't have had much fun there."

"I'd say not."

"Who was all there?" my mom said. She was folding some laundry in the living room. I took a quiet, deep breath. It was a conversation that I didn't want to have, but I knew it was inevitable.

"There was a four-star general there. I couldn't believe it."

"Four stars, huh?" she said, like she found it unlikely.

"Yeah, rough-looking dude. Gabe Fleming from ABC News was there, as well as Louis Mitchell, the former CIA Director."

My grandma was in her apron, working hard to clean up her bright, yellow kitchen. I remained parked at the dining room table, trying to speak politely while I devoured my pancakes.

"How do you know that?" my mom asked. "Did he tell you?"

"Yeah, at first, I didn't know who anyone was, so he told me later after some of them had left. There was a real nice woman there too who I met. It was odd because she was the only woman there." There was a long pause from my mom who stopped folding her towels.

"The only one, huh?" she said.

"Yeah. She was very sharp and engaging." Not sure where that came from, but whatever.

"Do you know why?"

I felt a scream coming on. "Do I know why what?"

"Why there was only one woman there." My mom glanced into the kitchen. I thought she wanted to explain herself without my grandma hearing.

"No, why?"

"Because she was the token woman."

Chapter Thirteen

The conversation with my mom was rather difficult. We never had the best communication, mostly because I lied a lot and never told her my true feelings about anything. I walked around like a human iceberg. I thought as soon as I could make it on my own, I'd figure out my problems, so I really didn't need the loads of advice that she'd been giving me.

In my defense, she really was like a broken record at times—she wouldn't give it a rest, ever. She was constantly in my ear, "You need to keep your eye out for stuff like that" or "You sound like your father when you say that" and "You want people to take you seriously." It never stopped. Then, there was her fascination with correct grammar. Thanks to her, I think I knew the difference between a verb and a noun right as I left the womb. It took many years, but eventually I realized that these lessons were her way of saying "I love you," just in the most annoying way possible.

In that talk, it was Eli Gibson and how he was bad for me or whatever. I didn't believe it. I figured, if I saw something I didn't like, I'd just walk away. Never did I think my life would be in danger, except for that one night with the whole terrorism driver's training thing. But besides that, it was just excitement. Having a cocktail now and then, or doing courier runs through the streets of D.C. in a sports car, or dining with gorgeous, classy brunettes, was loads of fun. I craved excitement. I just wanted to take it a step further. As a boy, I loved doing something forbidden or exciting and then ending up back on my front stoop to relive it for friends, especially the girls. It was somewhat about showing off, but also about the feeling you get when you discuss something that would otherwise get you in trouble.

So, once my mom was done smothering me with hot air about my studies and my character and whatnot, I had to ask: "Token woman?"

She had finished folding laundry and was at the dining room table, looking over some real estate paperwork. She put it down, took her glasses off, and stared at me with a certain determination, as though to draw me in.

"That's when a group of men who are gay have one woman show up because they are obligated to do so, not because she provides some value to the group. It's a sexist thing, and you need to watch out for that. It's apparent in the workforce and the gay community, as well."

"Wait, what?"

"Gay men will have a token woman with them, especially if they're closet gays."

"Really?" *My hunch may have been correct.*

I thought about what I'd seen the night before, and nowhere did I feel like anyone was gay, except for Mr. Gibson and the way he offered me that glass of wine. There was something a bit feminine in his step when he entered the room and saw me. It was just. . .weird. If it weren't apparent to him that I was straight, watching myself and Nora engaged in conversation surely cleared things up.

***

"You ready to get to work?"

Mr. Gibson and I were on our way to the elevator at the Foxhall early the next week. I pumped a fist to display my enthusiasm.

We walked off the elevator. I had to keep up with him. For a small-stepped guy, he sure was quick. I figured one of his stories was coming, so I didn't say anything.

"What my group needs is someone to handle random responsibilities, errands, deliveries, picking up people, dropping them off, runs to the airport, that kind of thing. Much like you've done already. Did you get out and study some of the neighborhoods like we discussed?"

"I did. And I'll continue to do so."

We stood over one of the Mercedes. I heard the doors unlock with a slight echo from the dark parking garage and got inside.

91

"You need a courier," I said.

"I suppose so, just without the bike. You'll be much better equipped with the Supra and the occasional Benz. And sometimes they'll be two-man jobs."

I instantly thought about my mom. *Jobs?* This would be crossing the line, and she would not be allowed to know any of it.

"Sounds time consuming."

"Not really. Only when we need you."

Then I thought about the money.

He stuck the key in the ignition and turned to look at me with his sharp, knife-like blue eyes and that mischievous grin. "The money's good too."

With that, he revved the engine of the Mercedes Benz 190 E and headed into Georgetown.

We picked up Q Street off the Sheridan Circle, and he punched the throttle as the cross streets buzzed by. He made a left onto 30th Street and began looking at addresses. It was near dusk, so finding the numbers proved difficult. He stopped in front of a brownstone with wrought-iron fencing that enclosed arborvitae shrubs on either side of the sidewalk. There was not a parking space to be had. A rude honk from a Cadillac behind us caused him to turn his attention into the rearview mirror and drive off.

"I don't like being rushed," he said. "We'll take a spin and come back. Once we get close, you'll have to jump out and go drop this off." He pulled a large envelope from the backseat and handed it to me.

"May I ask?"

He snapped his head at me as though I had some nerve. "May you ask what?"

"What are you getting me into?"

Mr. Gibson made his way back to 30th Street. "Some things we do are confidential and involve people who like their privacy. Pretty sure we went over this already, no? Really nothing to concern yourself with."

The sound of the automatic door locks was my cue. I opened the door and looked behind me down the street. There were no cars coming in either direction.

"Who am I asking for?"

"Just tell them it's a delivery from Mr. Gibson."

Once I knocked on the glass of the antique door, a studious-looking woman with short blonde hair came to answer.

"Hello. I have a delivery from Mr. Eli Gibson." That's all I said. I'll never forget the ghostly look on the woman's face when I handed her the envelope. She slammed the door. I hustled down the steps and back to the waiting car

Chapter Fourteen

I laid awake that night again. Sleep was becoming more and more of a precious commodity. I couldn't, for the life of me, figure out what had happened. Why did that woman act so startled when I mentioned Mr. Gibson's name? He wouldn't have me do his dirty work, would he? I thought about what he told me earlier—about how a lot of his clients were political officials that required privacy.

I slipped out the kitchen door and went up on the roof for a smoke. I could see the Jefferson Memorial clearly, and I contemplated how that damn town worked. I felt like I was part of something criminal. Maybe this is where anyone else would have reached their "thanks but no thanks" moment, but for me, I was just warming up. I had to know the truth about Eli Gibson.

***

"Be here Sunday at ten o'clock," Nora said over the phone. I was at work in one of the two phone booths inside the club's main foyer. Mr. Gibson required me to contact him every day, unless he stated otherwise. Often, it was Nora or Philip answering the phone, and whenever I would hear her voice, I would envision her sitting across from me in the limo when we visited the White House, the way she looked in the dark with the illuminated fountain sparkling behind her.

I had to work on Sunday, so I needed to switch my shift with someone. "That works," I said. "What should I be prepared for?" I don't know why I asked that, I think I just wanted to extend the conversation.

"A little picnic," she said. "Have a good day." And the line went dead.

My coworker Mark kicked the door of the phone booth open. He was sopping wet. "You feel like working sometime today, dickhead?"

"Really important call." I slid past him and grabbed a ticket from the stack before running to the next car under the portico. The rain was really coming down, and it was still quite warm for early October. I had turned eighteen and had now been invited to some sort of picnic with Mr. Gibson, and hopefully Nora. I parked the guest's Jaguar and did the usual sprint up the four flights of slippery, wooden stairs in a downpour. So many questions about Gibson and his entourage, I guess I would pull back another layer of the onion on Sunday.

***

It was minutes before ten on Sunday, and I pulled in the driveway of Mr. Gibson's Kalorama home.

Only Nora's BMW was in the drive. The doors were open on the carriage house out back, and only one car—the Audi Quattro—was there. I let myself in and immediately heard running water coming from upstairs. But not your typical running water in a home, more like a firehose. I stood under the chandelier and looked up the staircase of dark, polished wood.

The sound stopped.

"Hello?" I said up the stairs.

"Up here." I could hear water dripping. *Does she live here?*

I remember being almost spellbound. For a young man to even be around a woman as beautiful as Nora was hard enough. To be summoned by her, upstairs in that beautiful home, was sheer torture. "Are you decent?" *No reply.*

Nora, wearing a white terrycloth robe with a *Willard Hotel* crest, stepped out of the master bedroom and stood before me. She was ringing out her hair and looked full of energy. "You like horses, Calvin?" She smelled like honeysuckle, and her nails had a fresh coat of a merlot-colored polish.

"We're going to the track?"

"Heavens no." She crossed the hall into a guest room. "We're going to the polo grounds. Eli has a vested interest in one of the teams. But you're not going dressed like that." I looked at myself and felt somewhat inadequate. I had on khakis, a navy-blue polo, and my Doc Martens. Sporty, but certainly not ritzy. She came out of a walk-in closet with a light blue and white-striped seersucker suit on a hanger. She pulled it off the hanger and held it up to me.

"Try this on for me."

I did as she asked and found it too snug. She walked back into the guest room and fumbled around in the closet. She came back with another suit that was gray and white striped. I was in the master bedroom by then, leaning against a large armoire made of chestnut. Falling into another daydream, I wondered if she and I were alone. *One day.*

"What's with the plumbing in this place?" I said.

"The plumbing?"

"Yeah, was that the shower running when I got here?" I had slipped on the jacket, and it fit almost perfectly.

"Okay, the pants," she said, ignoring my question.

Without hesitation, I snapped the buckle loose and pulled off my khakis and placed them on the bench. The arousal was starting to take over. Thankfully, I had at least some self-control because that could've been embarrassing. I slipped on the slacks, and they fit. She walked over to me and pulled on the lapels. Looking up at me, she ran her hands inside and along the waistline. I tried to hide it with my eyes, but I was sure she could sense the vibrations running throughout my body.

"You wear it well," she said. Our eyes met just as the phone rang.

Nora went to the antique vanity and answered it.

"Yes?" After several seconds, she responded, "Forty minutes I'm guessing." She turned and looked me up and down. "I outfitted him, he looks proper." I had assumed she was speaking with Mr. Gibson, but I couldn't be sure. I walked into the master bathroom, just out of curiosity.

Nora hung up the phone.

"Did he buy this from the fire department?" I said, having propped open the glass-enclosed shower door to find at least half a dozen jets imbedded into the tile wall. There was a control panel on the wall outside the shower and another one inside, and the door was as thick as a shot glass.

She entered the room, still in her robe. My hunch was that flirting with her would only end in embarrassment. Nora was out of my league. She clearly had to have a powerful gentleman somewhere in the city.

"Close the door," she said.

I did as she asked, and she hit four or five buttons on the control panel. A slight rush of water from two of the smaller heads began to spray. *Nothing special*. A moment later, the large heads kicked on. They resembled something out of a Las Vegas fountain, only stronger. I stood in wonder. "Can you turn them all on?"

She pushed two more of the black buttons, and I noticed her laughing to herself. "He's in there for half an hour sometimes. Comes out looking like a lobster." All six jets were on full blast, and the shower room itself filled with steam. The room was all tile, beige in color, and there was a ledge on the left of the jets, perhaps for a person to sit and enjoy a steam bath. The flow of the water against the glass and the sound of the jets were soothing.

To think that my life's biggest crush, Nora, was in there just a while before and that she was standing before me now, still naked under her robe, was exhilarating. *Work for Gibson, seduce Nora. Isn't life grand?*

She turned the jets off. For a moment, the only sounds were the drips of the shower nozzles as she cracked the glass door open to let the steam out. "Alright, finish getting dressed," she said. "We'll be leaving soon."

"Sure thing." I walked through the master bedroom toward the hallway and remembered I had left some of my clothes on the bench at the foot of the bed. As I turned around, Nora slipped off her robe and walked into the closet. She caught my eye in the vanity mirror and didn't seem bothered at all. I gave her two quick glances. The first was the *I'm sorry* glance, and the second was a definite *thank you*.

Chapter Fifteen

We stopped at a local wine shop and specialty food store, right near the square in Potomac. Nora handed me a basket, and we made our way to the deli counter. I kind of felt like her butler—which I suppose I was to some degree—but at least she didn't make it obvious. She picked out some prepared sandwiches, a few different cheeses, and a small carton of olives. It was clear that she'd been shopping here for some time, as the employees said hello by name and catered to her with extra attention.

After grabbing a few bottles of wine, I reached for my wallet.

Nora smiled. "Nice gesture, but there's no need."

The clerk rang up our items, and Nora merely signed a bill—like it was a house account or something. The more time I spent around her and Mr. Gibson, the more they continued to surprise me. And now we were on our way to a picnic...at a polo match.

***

I had a hunch that some instructions would be coming my way, and I was right.

101

"Stay with the group," Nora said, as I drove down River Road. She was wearing a top shift, ivory-white dress with a brown, rope-like stitching across the front. It was both rustic and sporty. "There will most likely be a large crowd since it's the season's final match. Don't drink too much. Keep your jacket on. They'll serve food, but I like having our own on hand."

"So, act like a gentleman?"

Nora looked away from me. "Turn right here."

After what must've been a mile, a couple of young kids flagged us into a *reserved* parking lot behind the hospitality tents that sat close to the field. The Washington Polo Field was a vast, wide-open space, and there were at least a few hundred cars in the lot.

While pulling items out of the trunk, I spotted Mr. Gibson in a private tent, just off the large commercial tent for the public. *Of course, he has his own.* He whistled and waved at us, and Nora waved back. "Go ahead," I said. "I've got it."

Nora grabbed a cowboy hat that matched her dress. "You sure?"

"I think I can handle it."

Gathering our picnic items, I peered over the car and watched Nora enter the tent. Mr. Gibson held her hand up and bowed as his guests laughed and encouraged him. He then began the formalities of introducing Nora to the other guests. I couldn't spot any of his usual colleagues. There were a few young guests—two young men and a young woman. *Right, the callboys complete with a token.* There were several other men, one wearing a turban. I recognized him from the Foxhall. My grandma called him "The Jordanian Prince" and said that he had bought the entire tenth floor and turned it into one enormous penthouse. She had acted like they were old pals. I slammed the trunk. *Let's go see what we can learn today.*

The man from Jordan grabbed my arm. "I like for you today."

I yanked my arm away and looked at Nora for any kind of assistance. I was ready to direct him to the two other young men who were standing near Mr. Gibson, but I decided not to make it any more of an issue.

I walked past the group to a table dressed in a light blue cloth and put down the groceries.

"He's from overseas and was mistaken," Mr. Gibson said.

"Quite mistaken," I said. Mr. Gibson was probably feeling me out, wanting to know if he could bring me around to his parties like he does these other young men. The answer was clearly *no*. These people, although attractive, seemed dead to me. They had these blank stares, and I could see their dark pasts in the way they carried themselves. Something about them made me feel hollow. I began to wonder about Gibson. And that made me wonder about Nora.

Mr. Gibson looked at me with disappointment "There's no need for hostility."

"You haven't seen me hostile, Mr. Gibson."

The smoke from his cigar lingered in his mouth until the breeze slowly pulled it away. He stood in front of me in his white chinos and a gray checkered blazer and observed his entourage, who were all gathered around someone. I felt like I was ruining everyone's afternoon, but that wasn't the case. I was the courier and that was it, nothing more.

He turned his attention back to me. "I like you," he said. "You've got a confidence about you that—"

"Those guys don't have?" I motioned over to his callboys.

"I didn't say that."

"Mr. Gibson, you've been very generous, and I've enjoyed getting to know you and Nora and the others. And I want to stay on as your courier. But you've met my family, so I'm sure you understand my situation."

"Let me make it worth your while."

"You already have. But I'm the courier, Mr. Gibson, nothing else."

He laughed into his cigar, which caused him to cough. Once he recovered, his eyes were stinging red. "Right. The *courier*. But I also have a few events that could use some coordinating. Political events. You'd be working with Nora, and I know you don't mind that." I had to hand it to him, he did get me to smile. "We'll talk more about it this week. Now, let's grab a drink and see what all the fuss is about, shall we?"

***

The match was to start in less than an hour, which allowed us time to go see the horses, or as the patrons referred to them, the *ponies*. After pouring a few glasses of wine for Nora, Mr. Gibson, and myself, I noticed that Nora already had one and was being quite dazzled by one of the polo players, who had thick black hair and looks that you'd find in an in-flight magazine to Barcelona. It turned out that Gibson had a stake in this polo team, which included the purchase, care, and training of over two dozen ponies.

I was not introduced to Luis, the lavish polo player from Portugal, but we did share a polite glance. Nora had her arm under his as we walked to the corrals.

The young girl who was part of the entourage was walking next to me. She had dark red hair and swollen green eyes, as if she spent a lot of time crying.

"I've never seen you before," she said.

"Likewise."

"From around here?"

"I am now. Cleveland originally."

With an almost vocal emptiness, she said, "I'm from Kansas," and stared off as though she wished she'd never left.

I didn't get her name. My instincts told me she was a call girl for Gibson.

We arrived at the corrals to view the horses. Nora still clung to Luis, who was dressed in his polo uniform of a red *Coca-Cola* shirt and white pants. Mr. Gibson was speaking to the trainer and posing for a photograph. Him standing beside the horses, with a glass of wine and a cigar in one hand and the other draped around the trainer, is an image I'll never forget. He was a celebrity in my eyes. Nora leaned into Luis and smiled for the photographer. There must have been some romance between them in the past, and probably more in the future.

I motioned for the girl with green eyes to follow me over to one end of the corral. Nora was kissing one of the horses and laughing with Luis. She made a cracking sound with her mouth to get the horse to turn his head toward her, making me think she might have been raised around them.

"Which one do you like?" I asked the girl.

"They're all pretty."

"Ever been on one?"

"No," she said with contempt. I had struck a nerve, and she shot me a look that haunted me. I had a visual flash of her being tortured. It was like she wanted me to feel it, like a cry for help.

Just as I was about to speak, one of the young men came over to us. "Daphne, let's go," he said with a touch of drawl. No hesitation, no farewell, she simply walked away with him. And just like that, they

106

followed a few of Gibson's guests and were gone, on their way to who knows where.

On the walk back to the tent, I caught up to Nora. I watched as the group headed toward the cars. "They're not even sticking around to stomp the divots?" I said. Nora looked toward them and didn't say anything. For a moment, I thought about what the hell I was doing with those people. The problem was, I knew what I was after, and I knew that I was going to stick around.

"They have some other obligations," she said. "Don't concern yourself." I took that as an order.

The afternoon was filled with the excitement of the match, the rumbling of the horses' hooves as the players bared down on the ball. Ten horses with riders in bright colors flashed by and tried to position themselves for a strike. Although there was a nice breeze, it was warm for October, and the horses had to be rotated often. I found the halftime tradition of 'divot stomping' to be hilarious—everyone brought their drinks, and some women had umbrellas and hats to avoid the sun. And being that it was the last match of the year, it was a cause for excessive celebration.

I did make one observation that I found interesting: the man from Jordan snapped at the photographer, and Mr. Gibson got between them to offer some diplomacy. Obviously, the Prince did not want any pictures of himself with Mr. Gibson.

Chapter Sixteen

It was mid-November, and George H. W. Bush had just won the presidential election, much to the dismay of my aunt and uncle. My grandma, a Republican, had voted for the Democratic candidate, Michael Dukakis, probably just to please my Uncle Jack and for the sake of dinner table conversation. Regardless of whose party won, come late January, there would be an enormous transfer of power, celebrated with all the pomp and circumstance that the world could tolerate, led by the Inauguration of the 41st President of the United States on the West Capitol steps.

As January 20, 1989 approached, I had been in full swing of running courier errands for Mr. Gibson. On several occasions, his bodyguard—or whatever he was—Philip and I had picked up young men from the airport. They must've been instructed not to talk because they never said much.

There were a few young ladies too, all slim and attractive, but a little worn in the eyes, much like the red-haired girl at the polo match. It was usually after ten o'clock, which made it hard for me to keep coming up with excuses for not being home. I was working at the club about twice a week, but as for the ladies I lived with, they thought it was more like four. For daytime runs, I was signing myself out of school using the Age of Majority law, and if my mom found out, there would be hell to pay. My intuition about Mr. Gibson had so far been spot on, and after getting more involved, and the things that I had noticed, if he weren't running an escort service, then I was well off the mark. In fact, *escorts* would've been a compliment; these people were *prostitutes*.

Standing in National Airport with big, meathead Philip, holding a sign with some random name, which was probably fake anyway, made me uneasy but excited. It was like being in a gangster film; I enjoyed the rush. I figured if Philip ever decided to not like me, he could make my life hell. His physique, straight face, and dull personality made him seem like he didn't understand pain. He also knew how to follow orders, some of which I wouldn't want to know about.

On our way back from the Willard Hotel downtown, where we dropped off two scantily clad young ladies, he was in the passenger's seat of one of the Mercedes, shaking his head. "It'll slow down after the inauguration."

"What do you mean?" I said.

"All these airport runs. They'll slow way down."

"Oh, gotcha." He was such a lonely bastard. I didn't want to know any more about him than I already did. It was way too quiet on the ride back, so I had to ask. "Do you know Nora?"

He glanced at me. "Yeah."

Well, shit. I was hoping for more than that.

"We're supposed to have lunch soon."

Looking straight ahead, he sported a half grin on his bullish face. I sensed that he had tried to score with her and got shot down.

"You're a little too young for her," he said. "But be careful either way, she can make or break you."

I officially hated Philip.

***

My Aunt Emma was to co-host an inauguration party at the office of the Congressional Representative of Maryland. Ten Russian foreign exchange students visiting D.C. were invited to attend. Somewhere in her planning, she thought it would be a good idea if I would lead them safely to and from the ceremony. At that point, I didn't know what would be more exciting—escorting the Russians or attending with Mr. Gibson, Nora, and the rest of his entourage.

I couldn't turn my aunt down, so on the morning of January 20th, I left the Foxhall on foot to get downtown. Trying to get on the Metro on the day of the inauguration was a challenge, considering there were an extra 300,000 people in the city. It was not a good place for the claustrophobic. I sprinted down the stairs and slipped and dodged through people until I was close to the center of the platform. The conversations, some in different languages, police radios, and the horns and steel wheels of oncoming trains echoed throughout the dark, circular tunnel. It reminded me of how I thought the D.C. Metro was designed in the future. The first train that pulled in was nearly full, so I allowed others to board and waited for the next one.

The next train was packed as well, but I managed a standing position just inside the smooth-sliding metal doors. Perfume, coffee, and alcohol lingered in the train car. People were chatting it up, obviously energized to witness history. I was too. I thought about spending the morning with Nora. I imagined us reminiscing about it one day.

"So, where did the two of you meet?" some random person would ask. I would let her answer first.

"It was at the Dolley Madison. He called a week later to invite me to the inauguration."

"The rest is history," I'd say. Wouldn't that have been nice. I loved daydreaming on the train. The rhythmic motion and the sound of the steel wheels on the track were soothing, like a cat purring on your chest, only amplified.

"Next stop, Capitol South," the overhead voice said. There were subtle cheers in the car, as the anticipation of witnessing history was getting to people. I moved out of the way of the sliding doors so that others could depart before me. I had a flash of nervousness, so I took a deep breath. I had to remind myself that I could do what my Aunt Emma asked of me. An inner voice wanted to remind me that I was still just a troubled kid from Cleveland who wasn't cut out for this new life. I took another deep breath and moved quickly toward the crowd forming at the base of the stairs.

I made it to the Longworth House Office Building as quick as I could and found my Aunt Emma and Congresswoman Jane Mckyle. It wasn't long before the Russian students showed up—all ten of them. They were dressed in clothes that looked like they were hastily grabbed out of a Salvation Army dumpster, and their skin was so pale. If I could have walked them into a department store and outfitted them all in modern clothing, I would have. I envisioned them outside the Kremlin waiting for a bus in sixty below temperatures. None of them had the look of wonder or excitement about them, it was as though they were just doing their duty. Watching them made me sad, and I did my best not to stare.

The girls looked, well, *Russian*. One of them was blonde. She was quite tall and was wearing a thick, plaid blazer along with maroon corduroys. The bright blue mascara was a bit overdone, but she probably liked it, so I did too.

My aunt told me I would be sharing the responsibilities with a girl from Chevy Chase, the town next to Bethesda, her name was Claire. She smiled at me with rosy cheeks as I approached her.

112

"Are you Claire?"

She hid her gum. "You must be Calvin. Check out these seats." She had the tickets, a seating chart, and what looked like the instructions on how we were to get there. She handed them to me. The Russian kids were talking amongst themselves, leaning against the wall in the long hallway outside the congresswoman's office. Surprisingly, the seats were very close to the west front of the Capitol, where President-elect Bush would be sworn in, so we would be able to see everything.

"I can't believe this," I said. "I figured we'd be watching from Virginia."

Claire looked at me and laughed. "Good to know people, I guess. Or in your case, be related to them."

"Not sure I had a choice, but I'm glad I'm here now. You speak Russian?"

She whistled and motioned to the students to follow us into the congresswoman's office. "That's about it," she said.

I found my Aunt Emma when we entered the crowded room. There had to be fifty people in a room large enough to hold about half that many. I walked Claire over to her.

"Aunt Emma, this is Claire from Chevy Chase."

"Well, good morning, Miss Claire."

Claire smiled when she heard my aunt's southern drawl. "It's nice meeting you, Mrs. Gregory."

"Listen to me now. These kids have somewhere

113

to be this afternoon, so once the ceremony is over, you hustle them back to Friendship Heights, you hear me? Keep a head count and check it throughout the morning and once again on the train."

I didn't realize that we'd now be responsible for these kids on foot and by train as well. "We won't let you down, Aunt Emma," I said. "Thank you for including me. I think."

She smiled. "Make sure you pay attention. You're about to witness history." Her hair was a silvery-gray, and she had a sharp nose and big blue eyes. She was easily the best-dressed woman in the room, wearing a navy-blue dress with a shiny, silver necklace and a small American flag button on her lapel.

I took a stop by the refreshment stand and snagged a couple sugar cookies. While I ate them, I motioned to Claire that we should move out. What an odd-looking group we were. I looked like I was living two decades ahead of my new Russian counterparts. I was wearing gray slacks with a plaid button down and a red sweater-vest; it was about right for the cloudy, cool weather. I was dressed a bit more preppy than I would've liked, but I wanted to look sharp in case I ran into my new employers.

As we walked the few short blocks toward the Capitol, we were among a sea of people, and it was easy to get caught up in all the splendor. I turned around and faced the Russian students and made a motion with my

114

arms, as if to say, "Stay close together." Claire watched me and tried not to laugh.

"We lose one of them and I'm toast," I said.

"I think you're speaking for both of us."

"Suppose you're right."

There were steel barricades along First Street, and we passed several policemen, some standing outside their squad cars with the doors wide open, some on horseback. The horses looked like they had been groomed at Churchill Downs for the occasion. There were other security personnel using whistles and hand motions to try to control the crowd.

As our group entered a barricaded section, two men wearing sunglasses walked up on either side of me and motioned toward Fifth Street. "Come with us," one said. One placed his hand on my back as though he were guiding me away from danger or something. I was alarmed but made a quick, educated guess as to where they were from. *Gibson.*

I caught a glimpse of Claire and the blonde Russian girl as I began walking. Claire had her mouth open and looked scared. I was pretty frightened myself and thought about making a run for it. I held up a finger to Claire liked I'd be right back and then turned my attention to the two men.

"Can I help you, gentlemen?" Neither man acknowledged me; they just walked beside me and tried to navigate us through the crowd.

The shorter of the two said, "Mr. Gibson is requesting you."

"Oh, Jesus."

"Exactly. We've been following you since you got off the train."

We continued to dodge people until we reached a security gate. Three security personnel stood and checked badges and used metal detection wands on people as they admitted them into the Capitol. We were not even fifty yards from the East entrance, and it was less than an hour until the opening ceremonies.

Both guys were dressed in suits and had the same sunglasses on, both wearing badges, but I couldn't make out their full names. Once we were scanned by the metal detectors and patted down, we were next to enter. A large Capitol Hill guard looked at me and asked them, "Who's this cat?"

"He's with Gibson's group. Was supposed to be here earlier but got lost."

"I wasn't lost," I said. "I had another obligation, and Mr. Gibson knows that." I shot a look at both of my escorts and got no reaction.

"Okay, gentlemen, we'll see you back here in half an hour," the security guard said and ushered us in.

We finally reached our destination, inside the Capitol rotunda. It wasn't the first time I'd been inside the place, but on the morning of the inauguration, I was in awe. I forgot all about my obligations to the Russian students and my new friend Claire and just took a long

116

drink of the history. As a precaution, I looked around for my great-uncle, wondering what kind of awkward greeting he would have if he saw me there. It was as I was scanning the rotunda that I spotted Mr. Gibson, and behind him, the lovely Nora.

I followed the two men over to Gibson's gathering of about twenty people. His demeanor was not his usual. He was much more reserved and proper. It made me think he was one of those people who led two different lives, but by then that wasn't exactly a newsflash.

"Morning, sir."

"Calvin, my good man. I thought we'd missed you." We received a few stares from people in the group. I'm sure they all wondered who I was. I continued the small talk with Mr. Gibson and met a few of his colleagues, all the while keeping Nora in my sights. She wore an off-white raincoat over a medium-length red dress and a pearl necklace. Her silky dark brown hair was down, and I noticed her nail polish matched her dress. She flashed a little smile when she noticed me.

"Calvin. You made it." She winked at me. It was loud with the hundred or so people scattered around, and the rotunda made it into an echo chamber.

"Wouldn't miss it."

"Quite the patriot."

"I'm supposed to be escorting a dozen Russian students down here, but I got pulled away by the two goons." I motioned to the men who brought me to the Capitol building. "Do you know them?"

"They moonlight for Eli. Don't you need to get back? And where you're sitting?" I showed her my ticket along with the seating arrangement that my aunt had given me. After some more small talk and quick introductions with others, she walked me back to the door where I had entered and shared something with me that I'd never forget.

"Calvin, why didn't you tell me who your uncle was?"

I paused for a moment, "I didn't feel obligated," I said. "Eli knows."

"That's who told me."

I didn't say anything, I just looked out the door at the sea of people forming, all eagerly awaiting the president-elect of the United States to place his hand on the bible and raise his right hand. What a spectacle it was.

"And?"

"Oh, c'mon," she said with a sheepish smirk. "Your great-uncle is serving in the Senate and you act like it's no big deal?"

"You think it's a big deal? To Eli, I mean?"

We moved out of the way as a group of tourists walked past. "It will complicate things. I'm only warning you."

This was not the time or place that I wanted to have a conversation about my uncle. For all I knew, he

118

was about to pat me on the shoulder and ask how in the holy hell I got inside the Capitol rotunda. "Can we talk about this later?"

"Now is the time to remove yourself from all this, Calvin. A new president means a new administration and a new game in town." She got close and tugged at my jacket. "Sure, it's fun, but all good things must come to an end. Go quietly or you might ruffle the wrong feathers. Don't say I didn't warn you."

I took in a breath. Her brown eyes were both concerned and serious. In life, we have moments that we remember forever: the date, the weather, or the way a person looked. Nora created a moment for me that morning, one that I'll always try to remember. I looked beyond her, out toward the crowd, the unfolding of history, people as far as the eye could see.

"Let me sleep on it."

Chapter Seventeen

As quick as I could, I dodged and weaved through the crowd, thinking of what I would say to Claire. I caught up to the group just as they were entering through one of two security gates, maybe a hundred yards from the Capitol steps. I suppose that the first gate was to make sure people weren't carrying weapons or anything suspicious, and then the second one was *to really make sure*.

"Nice of you to make it back," Claire said. Her quick look away told me she was annoyed.

"A friend of the family. He doesn't take no for an answer. I've about had it with him."

"What did he want?"

"Believe it or not, his party was in the rotunda. I think he was just showing off." I was looking forward to changing the subject. "Any way we could keep this between us?"

"Oh, we're keeping secrets now? This friendship is really picking up steam."

"I'm sorry."

That afternoon, there were hundreds of police officers, some on horseback, but mostly on foot. There were barricades and squad cars, some unmarked, that blocked off Pennsylvania Avenue, the route that the president and his wife would take walking back to the White House. *Maybe Mr. Gibson would be invited to one of the Inaugural Balls later…or better yet, maybe the White House.*

The time had arrived. George Herbert Walker Bush was being sworn in as the 41st President of the United States, right before our very eyes. He used the same bible that President Lincoln had used. He wore a black suit and overcoat with a silver tie, and his wife Barbara wore her familiar pearl necklace and blue overcoat. There was music from the Marine Corps Band and a packed crowd from the west steps all the way to the Tidal Basin. President Reagan and First Lady Nancy were there. The president's family was all in attendance, as well as Vice President Dan Quayle.

As the president-elect walked out of the rotunda and toward the Capitol steps, I watched him closely. He shook many hands and shared a few laughs. I was taking everything in, watching in awe. Thinking it couldn't become any more of a spectacle, Mr. Gibson gave President-elect Bush a firm handshake, and the two men stopped and shared a few words. People moved out of the way while the Secret Service stood around them. Finally, they turned toward a waiting cameraman, and both smiled for two shots.

I can still see him with his hand on the bible. "I, George Herbert Walker Bush." I liked him. He was a Navy bomber pilot in the Pacific during World War II and a great American. He had been Director of the CIA before he was chosen as President Reagan's running mate, another man I admired. *The Gipper*. The same man who was waiting patiently to transfer the executive powers over to his successor. And now that Gibson somehow had ties to both men, I was trembling with excitement.

President-elect Bush had been groomed for this for years. The fact that Michael Dukakis could be standing up there threw me for a loop. I couldn't even imagine it. Ever since seeing him posing in an Army tank during a commercial, I just had a hard time taking him seriously as a candidate.

After a frantic scramble of getting the students back to Friendship Heights and getting myself to Maggie's Pizza with my fake I.D., was I able to relax. I made it home just before dusk and hit the rooftop for a smoke. There was a lot to consider and to let sink in. Thinking about what Nora had said, I was glad I preferred to keep my options open. Witnessing the handshake between Bush and Gibson had left me speechless. I knew my life would change coming to Washington, but gazing out at the Lincoln Memorial that night, one word kept coming to mind:

Duty.

ACT II

Chapter Eighteen

"Corruption is worse than prostitution. The latter might endanger the morals of an individual, the former invariably endangers the morals of the entire country."
– Karl Kraus

My desire to see Nora grew by the day. Maybe a spontaneous visit to Capitol Hill to have lunch with my Uncle Jack would serve as good reason to be in the neighborhood. The twist would be that I would just stop by and say a quick hello, drop off some pastries or something. From there, I would stop by Nora's office and ask her to lunch. There wasn't much risk, besides missing school, but it's not like Uncle Jack would be checking up on me. I planned to lie and say my visit was for a class research project; he would buy that. Lying to a U.S. Senator couldn't be all that difficult, right? I had a good vibe about this, plus using the Age of Majority all but guaranteed my afternoon off.

In my young life, I had never been naked with a classy, dignified, and seductive woman like Nora, and I was determined to see it through. This wouldn't be a quick shack-up either since *fucking is for amateurs*, as someone told me once. We would get a room at the Willard or the Dolley most likely, at least that's what I was envisioning. I knew she ran with some big hitters. There was betrayal, blackmail, hush money, forbidden secrets, and all that. She was the queen of hearts, and I was going all in.

Visions of the two of us jetting off to southern France or somewhere with Mr. Gibson and his dignitaries, where I would train in counter terrorism and Nora could broker deals for Gibson, it was all right there in front of us. We would visit the fine vineyards, ski in the Alps, and play baccarat in the casinos of Monte Carlo. I was quite delusional, but it all seemed possible.

My Uncle Jack's office was in the Dirksen Building, which was on the northeast corner of the Capitol. It was constructed after World War II, when the government decided to start growing into the monstrosity that it is today. They even had their own subway system to the Capitol underneath the office buildings.

When I had visited him there a few years prior, we took the *monorail* to the Senate Dining Room for lunch. Maybe for anyone else, this wouldn't be that big of a deal, but to me it was the trip of a lifetime. I took the Metro down to the Hill that day. I dressed up a bit but nixed the tie. I wore a dark gray pair of slacks, a blue dress shirt, and a dark blue blazer.

I had become a stickler about my shoes, and this pair was one that I was particularly proud of: my Bostonian wing tips, or "Brogues" as they're called in England. The wingtip is nothing but a shoe to most men, but I took a liking to history, and it turned out that the wingtip was from Scotland, which was part of my roots. The idea behind the perforations, which ran all the way through the leather, was to let the shoe breathe in case a man had to wade through a stream or something. Either way, I looked sharp that afternoon, but maybe a little too much like a staffer.

I arrived at the entrance to the Dirksen Building, named after the late Senator of Illinois, *Everett McKinley Dirksen*, who was famously quoted in 1964 as saying that racial integration was "an idea whose time had come." Why those words aren't etched in granite somewhere is a real shame. The entrance to the seven-story building is near unforgettable, as the doors are made of thick, heavy bronze. Inside, the building is faced in marble with an American Eagle sculpture in the center, and above the glass windows were spandrels of symbols for shipping, farming, mining, manufacturing, and lumbering, those livelihoods this city seemed to be working diligently to destroy.

I walked down about ten hallways. One of my weaknesses was getting lost in buildings, especially a big, important one like the Dirksen. A few quick turns, an elevator ride, and before I knew it, I was lost. I ended up stumbling upon his office after turning a corner, and there it was, with the infamous sign out front: The Honorable Senator Jack Gregory. *Honorable…right.*

Actually, if anyone in that town *was* honorable, it was my Uncle Jack.

I waltzed right in like I owned the place, and I asked the first person I saw, some young female staffer, "Is my Uncle Jack in?" I remember at least five heads turned. That wasn't something anyone in that office heard often. They were used to "senator," and "senator" only. *Forgive me.* I'm the guy who just mowed his lawn. Besides, I was hoping he wasn't there, so I could run over to Nora's office, before the lunch hour anyway.

Low and behold, the Senator was in. S*hit*. He came walking out of his back office dictating some important matter to his chief of staff, a woman named Leslie Starr. She was great looking: a short brunette with big, blue eyes. She also had a classy southern drawl. She was always super nice to our family.

"Well, my word, Calvin. Haven't you just grown right on up," she said to what was now a roomful of laughter and awkwardness. Not long ago, I would have blushed and looked at the ground for a second before recovering, but times had changed.

"That's quite kind of you, Miss Leslie, great seeing you." I found it funny how a lot of us in my family could assimilate a drawl when in the presence of sons and daughters of Dixie.

By now, Uncle Jack was out in the lobby and seemed less than impressed that I'd stopped by. He did his usual folksy head turn and said with the utmost sincerity, "What brings you down to the Hill today, son?"

"You all look busy."

He found what I said hilarious, and when he laughed, his smile resembled a slice of watermelon—easily the biggest smile in the Senate. If you saw a photo of him from back when he was campaigning, you'd do a double take just to gaze at his smile.

"A few of us were going to have a little lunch over in the Senate Dining Room," he said. His folksy drawl and soft voice could stop you in your tracks. "Now, being that you've come dressed better than you were when Reagan was in office, would you care to join us?" We laughed again, and I was impressed by his sharp memory.

Uncle Jack had taken my grandma, mom, sister, and myself to the Senate Dining Room once before. I was probably fifteen at the time and couldn't have felt more out of place. On that occasion, I had showed up without a dinner jacket. My Uncle Jack seemed perplexed on what to do and started asking people whether they would let us in the Dining Room. The kid from Cleveland was there to visit his uncle in the Senate, and he wasn't dressed properly. I felt ashamed, like I shouldn't have been there in the first place. After a quick call to Leslie Star, she said to ask the coat check for one we could borrow, which we did. The jacket didn't match my clothes, and it didn't fit much better.

During our lunch that day, my Uncle Jack kept getting approached by other senators whispering in his ear. I kept imagining they were making jokes about my jacket, that's how much the whole situation bothered me.

After reminiscing about my prior visit, I fed him some line and politely declined. I looked at my watch: it was getting close to noon, and I needed to get a move on, since my fantasy lover, Nora, was waiting. She wasn't really waiting at all, the whole day was a crapshoot, but I didn't care. I was dressed sharp, had a few hundred bucks on me, and was on Capitol Hill, just taking it all in.

Nora was working for one of Washington's most elite PR firms, Ingersoll & Mather. She had been there for about three years and was trying to move into PR within the defense contracting industry. This made her even more appealing. Her office was on 19th Street, a half-mile walk from the Dirksen building, giving me a few minutes to work out the butterflies. Traffic was dense and moving slowly on that brisk early spring day. Most tourists were on foot while cabs, buses, and cars with out-of-state license plates packed the streets. I told myself not to reveal my schoolboy crush. I *just happened to be in the neighborhood*.

It was an attractive building, with glass running the length of each of its twelve floors. I imagined Nora getting off the Metro and doing a sexy, professional walk to the entrance where, no doubt, some gentleman would be there to open the door for her. *He'd better*. The lobby was large and had dark, marble floors and an enormous bronze chandelier in the center. The windows out front stood as tall as the room itself, so it gave off warm rays of sunlight on what was left of the morning.

I took the elevator to the tenth floor and, luckily, was by myself for a moment. As the elevator moved up, I looked at my reflection in the brass plate over the fire extinguisher, like I often did at Foxhall. This was mostly to make sure that my cowlick wasn't presenting itself, which it was, but barely noticeable. I took in a deep breath and exhaled as the elevator produced the familiar stomach-drop feeling, which meant it was showtime.

The Ingersoll offices were just down the hall, so there was one last chance to gather my thoughts and take a deep breath. I practiced my routine one more time:

Hi there, is Nora Dalton in, by chance?
Hello, is this Nora Dalton's office?
Good morning, what are the chances Nora...
Just shut up.

I found the double doors for Ingersoll & Mather Public Relations and turned the large, brass handle doorknob. Inside, there was a half-moon-shaped reception counter with two women sitting behind it. The one closest to me was talking on the phone. The other looked at me and gave me a pleasant, "Good morning, welcome to Ingersoll and Mather."

"By chance, is this Nora Dalton's office?"

"It is indeed. Unfortunately, Miss Dalton is out of town until tomorrow, may I ask who's inquiring?" As the woman was speaking, I noticed a man with a beard standing in the doorway of an office. He stopped what he was doing and turned toward us.

"I just happened to be in the neighborhood, so no big deal. I'm Calvin, and your name?"

"I'm Judy, Calvin. One of the office managers here. Would you like to leave a note in her mailbox?"

"That'd be great." By now, the man in the office doorway was joined by another man, and they were both looking at me.

I took the pen that Judy provided and wrote the following:

130

Nora-
Thought I'd surprise you for lunch today.
I happened to be down on the Hill.
Hope to see you soon.
Regards,
Calvin Ducane

I said my goodbyes to Judy, who was quite cute herself. She had a sort of 1950's-flight-attendant look to her, with sandy blonde hair and ruby-red lipstick. It seemed like wherever these people went, looks were important. I made my way out for what would be a long, deflated walk back to the Metro.

Was one of those guys who had been staring at me Nora's boyfriend? Would make sense, considering they all worked together. While the idea made me a touch jealous, I was open to a little competition.

Chapter Nineteen

The weekend arrived, and I went looking for the wicked Mr. Gibson. I told my mom that I was going to Georgetown to "bum around," and instead I took my usual route to the third floor. Sure enough, he was home. The door was open as usual, and he was in his office, on the phone. I let myself in and stood quietly in the living room, looking at a piece of art while I eavesdropped.

"Raymond, listen to me. They don't know. I'll make a few calls and we'll be back in business. Relax. They've got bigger fish to fry, trust me." He propped his feet upon the desk and twirled the phone cord in his hand. "No! You're serving your country, young man. You should be proud. I'll be back on the twenty-ninth. Let's have dinner before I leave. Tomorrow? Alright then, ta-ta for now."

Ta-ta for now? Who the hell says that?

He hung up the phone. "How are you, chap?"

That was better than "son" I suppose, but it gave me the feeling that I should be selling newspapers on the corner.

"What's been going on?" I said.

He looked awful. *Rode hard and put away wet*, as my uncle would say. He was still in a housecoat, and it was almost noon. His condo looked like it hadn't been cleaned in some time. There were clues there, no doubt. I just needed to look for them.

"I've been out of the country."

"Anywhere interesting?" A cigar magazine rested on his desk. I picked it up and sat down.

"Europe, tending to some business. I'll be leaving again soon." His tone was strange, as though he wasn't quite sure, or he was lying. "Some people that are looking for me, and it's best that I'm not around."

Aha! Today was going to be the day that he spilled the beans. I got comfortable in the leather chair facing his desk. Cigar smoke and day-old cologne filled the room.

"What people?"

"Can't discuss it right now."

There was a small mattress on the floor next to his desk with a fitted white sheet and a light blue blanket. You would trip over it if you tried walking along the side closest to the mirrored wall.

"Can you get me some dope?" he said matter-of-factly.

Oh, here we go. I fought the grin that was forming on my face. "Depends how much, I guess."

"What have you been doing? School good?"

I was still caught up in his previous question and finally came to. "School is rough right now. I'm not into it."

"You don't say."

I was still thinking about the dope. "Yeah, plus my uncle took the truck back, found a beer can…that kind of sucked."

"Oh no, how embarrassing."

It really wasn't embarrassing; it was more of a pain in the ass. Just because there was a beer can in the truck didn't mean I was out joyriding drunk.

"So, how much dope?" I said.

"As much as you can get. You need some money I suppose."

He grabbed an envelope off the desk. Underneath it was a razor blade and some remnants of coke. He took out a wad of cash that could fill a bank drawer. He peeled off five hundred-dollar bills and tossed them on the desk. They were crisp, brand new, and I could already smell them.

"I'll see what I can do."

"Splendid. Care for a drink?" He stood up and navigated his way around the mattress.

"I'll pass. Not much of a day drinker."

"Suit yourself." He poured vodka liberally over cracked ice. He motioned to the bed. "Too many guests last night, ran out of room."

God, I hope that's all it was.

I wished Nora was there. He looked like he hadn't slept. Maybe she could clue me in on what I had missed. He all but collapsed into the desk chair, his eyes sagging and his mouth hanging half open. He really needed to drop the curtain on this latest run.

"I went down to visit Nora in her office the other day," I said, hoping to distract him.

He sprang forward in his chair and began coughing. "What? When?"

"Last Tuesday. I happened to be down there during the lunch hour, decided to stop in. I missed her though."

"The lovely Nora. Isn't she something? She's making quite a career for herself down there. Does quite a bit for me too."

"She does?"

I got a long stare from his coked-out eyes. "Stick with me, son, and I'll make you a millionaire," he said again, just like when I had first met him. There was a long silence. "Son, after I left Vietnam, I moved to Japan to get involved in international business."

Fucking finally! He somehow went from drunken, coked-up party boy to dignified lecturer in the blink of an eye. "After a few tough years lost in translation and working for a lobbyist, I befriended the Mayor of Tokyo. We established a great business relationship. Great enough for me to entertain some of Washington's elite. I'm what they call a *powerbroker*, son. Politics, Hollywood, it's all the same. Gerald Ford, Ronald Reagan, Gabe Fleming, the list goes on. They're all my clients. So, you stick with me, son, I'll make you richer than you've ever imagined."

As strange as it sounds, I believed him. But only to a certain degree. It wasn't his connections that I questioned, it was his character.

"Is Nora single?" I asked.

"Sex on the brain, eh? Nora is an independent woman. She'll never be tied down. Too much of a career gal. And you're bush league when it comes to her."

That remark stung something fierce, but I wasn't about to argue. He didn't want to discuss Nora, which made me think that the 'token woman' thing that my mom had mentioned was true. *Might be kind of tough to get a gay guy to go to bat for you about a woman who's what, a call girl? Is that what she was moonlighting as?* All this mystery about her made me want her even more.

"Can I borrow the Audi?" I don't even know where that came from. I just blurted it out.

After an awkward pause he said, "You can't necessarily *borrow* the Audi, son…but you can *keep* the Supra. How's that?"

"Say again?"

"You can keep it so long as I live here, under one condition. Nobody knows whose car it is, just say it belongs to your family. Like I said, some people are more interested in me than I am in them." He swiveled in his chair and threw the keys across the desk at me. I didn't ask any other questions. Thoughts of burning down River Road with Nora in the Supra made me shake with excitement. I needed to get the hell out of there before he changed his mind.

***

"What size are you, son?"

"Size?"

"Well, you're not going to take Nora out with that awful jacket you wore before." He got up and started walking toward the hallway across the living room. I didn't know what to expect, but I followed him anyway.

We walked into a long closet that had to be twelve paces in length. There was row after row of suits, shirts, pants, all on wooden hangers, from formal black to a light-summer beige. There were pairs of shoes on the floor made of leather and filled with shoe trees; there were two-toned brown, dark brown and black ones and even an ivory-colored pair. There was an assortment of neckties as well, beautiful designs, all organized by color. Belts with shiny brass buckles, suspenders, cufflinks inside small, opened, black velvet jewelry boxes. There were gangster-type hats, Italian casual hats, all in a row on mannequin heads. There must've been a hundred dress shirts. They were nearly all white with a delicate shine and stiff collar, like they'd never been worn.

As he stood there, mulling over something, I took in the smell of leather and his rare cologne. I never got the gumption to ask him about the cologne; it seemed too personal and awkward. You ask a guy back on the old block what cologne he wears, you'll probably get a good kidney punch and gay jokes until the next school year.

"Here." He snapped a jacket off a hanger and opened it. "Turn around."

This must be how gay men play dress up.

At the time, I was wearing a golf shirt, blue jeans, and Doc Martens. I doubt I could have fit into any of his clothes, as he was smaller than me, but maybe there were clothes that belonged to someone else there, maybe this Raymond who had been on the phone.

Having been captured by the sight and smell of this room and its contents made me question my own sexuality. *Is it gay to like fine clothing? Has that been my problem all along?* If that were the case, it couldn't explain why I was so attracted to women, having lost my virginity at fourteen and rarely slowing down since. Girls, not women. Not yet anyway. Nora would change all that. I wanted to be with her on the rooftop of the Foxhall. I wanted to borrow Mr. Gibson's condo when he left town and have a romp session, in every room, on every surface. I wanted to douse her naked body in whiskey and seduce her to Journey, the Stones, and Fleetwood Mac. Ok, I wasn't gay. That settled that. And maybe not Journey. Maybe Led Zeppelin.

Although my sexuality was no longer in question, Gibson was gay. Not only that, it was obvious that he was testing the waters to see where I fit on the spectrum.

I was now standing in front of one of the mirrors that were on either side of the closet. *There sure were a lot of mirrors in this place.* The jacket was too long. *Hmmm, Raymond must be tall?* I was hoping there might be another option.

"Nope," he said. He didn't seem phased by this at all, since he had what seemed like fifty other jackets to choose from. *If all these jackets and suits averaged a thousand bucks a piece, what is the inventory in here?* It had to be a quarter million, including the shoes and trinkets. He snapped another jacket off its wooden hanger. That must've been something an Italian tailor taught him because he did it with vigor. I

138

suppose if he'd cleaned up his act and not been fresh off a coke bender, he would've looked much more stylish.

I turned around and stuck out my right arm to don the jacket. It felt different than the other. It was softer. As my biceps pulled the top of the jacket into place, he was standing right behind me, and I could feel and smell his breath on me. He gripped my shoulders and then pulled down on the sides of the jacket itself, giving me a sensation that I believe women call *the creeps*.

"This one looks good, son," he said in a low, gravelly voice that smelled of booze.

"I'm not so sure that it's the right fit." I said it in a tone to perhaps have him back away. He got the message. I wasn't hostile, but I was on full alert. If he had some strange ideas in mind, well, he picked the wrong guy. No harm, no foul.

"Turn around again, let's have a look at you." I looked in the mirror while he stood behind me. The jacket fit beautifully. I reached my right arm out, as if to shake hands, trying to picture if my shirt sleeve would extend properly.

"It's a great fit," he said. "Have you got a shirt?"

"Yeah."

"A fitted shirt…an Italian cotton fitted shirt?" He was having fun, hungover in his housecoat. "Hasn't Grandmama bought you some nice shirts to wear to Kennedy?"

I had made the mistake of trying to impress him when we first met and shared how I'd been to the opera at the Kennedy Center for the Performing Arts. I'd been there twice with my family and had fallen asleep during the Nutcracker. The intermissions were more interesting to me, where I somehow got served a rum and coke.

By this time, I had already slipped out of the jacket, which was made by a company called *Hugo Boss*, which my sister Samantha said was top notch. It had to be, since nothing ever fit me like that jacket did. He had me try on at least four different shirts. I didn't understand why the end of the sleeves were so long and stiff, but that's how they were designed so you could fold them and secure them with cufflinks. I did own a pair that my mom gave me. They weren't the antique style that he liked to brag about, but they were still nice. For a kid who was used to blue jeans and T-shirts, it was fun to dress like a ladies' man for once.

Finally, we found one that fit. We had been in this closet now for what seemed like an hour. I was getting hungry and was looking forward to taking the 500 bucks he'd given me to play drug dealer. Although I was technically involved in illegal activity, in my mind, I was only acting a part. That's how I saw it anyway.

"We're almost done here." He hung up the remaining shirts and jackets. "What do you think so far, son?"

"I've got to ask, why is it you keep referring to me as *son*?"

He gave me a peculiar look and a half smile. "Well, I hadn't thought about it. Would you prefer 'chap' or something else?"

140

"No, it's just that ever since I looked at that picture on your shelf in the office…." The pitch of my voice raised slightly, giving away my mild embarrassment.

"He's my son. Please don't be confused."

"I am confused. Where is he?"

His speech and tone slowed down as he looked past me. "He's studying in the south of France. Wants to be an architect someday. Don't worry, you'll meet him."

"He looks like my twin."

"You think? Let's finish up and go have a look, shall we?" He remained calm and happy, almost sober.

We picked out two ties, plus a pair of slacks that needed some mending to fit me, and then went into the office. He told me a brief story about his so-called *son*. "While I was in Vietnam, I met a girl who was in the Air Force, and before you knew it…."

I let him speak and didn't pry. He seemed so convincing.

"It wasn't meant to be, and we both led busy lives, so we decided we'd keep in contact for the good of Oliver."

Oliver. Oliver Gibson. My long, lost twin. How bizarre.

Either Mr. Gibson was telling me the truth, or he was a fantastic liar. I took another long look at the photo and then placed it right back where I'd found it, resting next to the one of Mr. Gibson and President Reagan.

Chapter Twenty

I left Mr. Gibson's without thinking everything through, and I walked into my grandma's condo having forgotten about my new outfit. She was just coming down the stairs, which was no easy task for her, bless her heart. Grandma was a swimmer. even then, in her seventies. she'd swim a mile a day. It was more like a quarter mile, but if you tried to argue that, well, you might want to put on a pot of coffee.

I could hear her humming as I opened the door. She stood on the staircase, looking me up and down in my new jacket, slacks, and tie along with my brown Doc Martens.

"Well, look at you," she said. "Don't you look handsome."

"Who's handsome?" I heard from upstairs. *Shit.* My mom came to the top of the stairs. She could see I had changed clothes, as I held my golf shirt and blue jeans under my arm.

"Wow," my mom said in a sarcastic tone. "I'm curious to know where that ensemble came from, but I think I already know. I thought you were going to Georgetown."

"I was…but I ran into Mr. Gibson in the lobby."

"Well, please explain."

"What, the clothes? He gave them to me after I told him I was going on a date."

My mom studied me up and down, said nothing, and then walked upstairs.

"I think you look handsome as all get out," my grandma said. "I don't know what's eating her."

I walked into the guest bathroom to have a look at myself. The jacket fit perfectly. It made me wonder if it had ever belonged to the kid in the picture. *Who was he really?*

I stood in front of the mirror and took out the five hundred-dollar bills from my pocket. I ran them along the edge of the counter to smooth them out. They had to be brand new, as though they'd left the printing press that very day. I gave them a smell. Mr. Gibson had given me that much money either to impress me or to lure me in. I was afraid I was falling for both.

***

Roshan and I were both scheduled to work that night, so we'd most likely be shooting craps in the valet room and betting on putts after dark. Plus, I had the keys to the Supra, so that night was setting up handsomely. The only way it could improve was if I got to see Nora, but that seemed unlikely.

I punched the throttle of the Supra and motored down River Road. As much as I liked the speed, it was the tight corners in areas like the Rock Creek Park, Cabin John, and Foggy Bottom where the Supra showed her stuff.

"I can't believe this fucking car," Roshan said.

"One of the perks of the job."

"Let me get this straight. Some dude who barely knows you, who has gay hookers and coke in his condo, a fleet of luxury cars…so, you wreck his car, caddie for him, and now you're wearing his clothes and driving his sports car?"

I took the opposite lane on Goldsboro Road to pass a car.

Roshan seized the leather seat. "Whoa!"

"Just testing out the acceleration."

We took MacArthur Boulevard back to Cabin John and made it back to the club in record time. Roshan pounded his head on the cafeteria table. "This is unbelievable. Is there a hot daughter too?"

"A son, actually, but he lives in the south of France."

"Oh, of course…the south of France."

"It's true. And Gibson wants me to move there after high school, right after we purchase the fish hatchery in El Salvador."

"Alright, stop. You're nuts. People just don't hand over stuff like that. Are you gay, Squire?"

"That's not it. I mean, I'm pretty sure he's gay, but not everybody in his group is. They seem to be your garden variety sex cult or something. But it gets better." I tossed my wallet over to him.

Roshan opened it, and his eyes grew big, making him look like a barn owl. He put the wallet down and whispered, "Are you serious?" He opened the wallet again and started counting. "One hundred, two hundred, three…holy shit."

I sat back in the booth and just shrugged my shoulders. I had no rhyme or reason for any of what I was involved in, except for my curiosity. Meanwhile, my life at home was questionable, and I'd been falling behind in my classes.

Roshan leaned forward in the booth. "You running drugs, Squire?" His sincere conviction got me nervous.

"I saw a picture of him with President Reagan on his mantel and—"

"So what?" he said. "Your uncle is a senator."

"Great-uncle."

"Something isn't right. I don't know, Squire, I'd be careful if I were you. I've never even met the guy, and I can tell that something's not right about him. Drugs and hookers look like fun in the movies, but that's a short life in the real world. You'd better watch your ass." He shook the ice in his plastic cup and finished the last of his soda.

"I am. I mean, I don't feel like I'm in any danger."

Roshan had heard enough. He started to scoot out of the booth. I put my wallet back in my pocket and cleaned up our mess. Roshan got up from the table and looked at me.

"So, what are you going to do with all that cash?"

I followed him to the soda dispenser. "Buy him a bag of weed."

Roshan laughed. "A big one."

Chapter Twenty-one

I had one more important errand to run, and that was to get Mr. Gibson his dope. If I were in Cleveland, it would be as easy as a code word or phone call, but I was unsure about this town, and I didn't know how much the guy wanted.

Greg Dorsey, who was another Whitman acquaintance, met me after work at Gina's Pizza—it was getting close to midnight.

I parked the Supra right out front to keep my eye on it.

"Is that your car?" he said.

"I wish. Just a work car."

A heavy-set guy with a head that didn't match, Greg wasn't much for friendliness. For a stoner, he dressed preppy, which was the trend. Khakis and penny loafers.

"Where are you working?"

"Just some work for someone in the city. Afraid I can't share any more."

A slight roll of his eyes made me want to get our deal over with. I couldn't blame him for his passive aggression, but there was no point in showing off. We had a beer and small talk, and then I met him out behind the building by his car.

"You want to try it out?" he said.

"Do I need to?" Being that I was the new kid in school, I suppose it would've been easy for him to try to screw me over. On the other hand, the rumors were out there, and maybe the consensus was to not mess with me. I wasn't sure, but I didn't want to get high in the city, in Gibson's car, and risk getting pulled over. When it came to street drugs, I could take them or leave them. I was a drinker.

We did our exchange and called it a night. I didn't even look at the contents. My goal was just to get home and hide the damn thing. It cost two-hundred bucks, and that was enough to fill a large freezer bag. I discovered that when you have something illegal in a car that doesn't belong to you, your whole thought process changes. I pulled over on a side street and put the weed in the trunk, stuffing it inside one of Gibson's golf shoes. I was looking forward to delivering on my promise.

Here's your dope, Mr. Gibson.

***

"Hi, Mom, I'm still at work. Hopefully get out of here by eleven or so."

"You know it's a school night, so you'd better hustle."

I was standing inside one of the phone booths in the Congressional lobby. Our shift was about over, but I wanted to buy a little time to pay the man a visit.

Twenty minutes later, I walked into Mr. Gibson's. By then, I was starting to have second thoughts about military academies. I was thinking more about joining up and going over to Europe for airborne school in Italy and then maybe joining an infantry unit in Germany.

Throughout our conversations over the past few months, Mr. Gibson had referenced some Delta force unit that was to be involved in the El Salvador project that he was lobbying for. These conversations gave me a real sense of purpose. I could see myself in that type of outfit. A Delta Force unit, El Salvador, fast cars, fast women—it felt like a dangerous lifestyle, and I liked the idea.

Mr. Gibson was tired when I walked in unannounced. He barely mustered up a greeting. Someone had cleaned the place, thank god. I was hoping it was Nora, but that kind of job wouldn't have been reserved for her. She was busy with much more important affairs.

"You up for a drink?" I asked.

"Help yourself."

"Can I get you a scotch or something?" This is what I loved about visiting Mr. Gibson. I was a player. I dressed well, drank expensive wine and gin and, more recently, took a liking to cigars. Cubans, so he claimed.

"A scotch would be nice," he said. I poured his scotch, twenty-five-year-old something or other, from the Waterford crystal. I made myself a stiff Bombay Sapphire and tonic. He kept the small, seven-ounce bottles of tonic that made for a perfect drink. I cut off the brown end of a lime and squeezed the rest into my glass and walked the drinks out into the living room. Mr. Gibson was seated on the couch on the side of the room closest to the office where the mirror hung the length of the wall. I sat across the room from him and got into my gin.

"You find any dope?" he said.

"Funny you should ask."

He perked up quickly. "Where'd you get it?"

"I don't divulge my connections, Mr. Gibson."

"Well, bring it over here, for God's sake."

I simply tossed it across the coffee table onto the couch. He grabbed it and unrolled it, pulling the bag open.

"This isn't dope!"

"What?" My face turned hot. "The hell is it then?"

"This is marijuana. I wanted coke. I thought I was clear?"

"Well, if you said 'coke,' then I guess that's what you'd be holding." I wasn't into cocaine. I had tried it, but it made my heart race and made me drink copious amounts of water. Not fun at all. "I'll find you some. I only spent part of the money you gave me anyway."

"Never mind," He got up and walked off.

I had two rolling papers in my wallet, so I started twisting a joint while he was his office. He was gone a good minute and came back smoking a cigar and brought an ashtray. I lit up the joint, took a drag, and then passed it to him. He hit the joint like a freshman, quick and awkward, then went into a violent cough.

"Jesus!" The veins in his skinny neck were standing at attention, and his eyes welled up with redness and tears. "Get that cheap shit away from me."

I laughed at him. I stood up and faced the mirror, taking in a drag. I looked out of place. Pot was one of those things that I did in my youth, but it was more so because of the environment that I was in. I really could take it or leave it. Mr. Gibson got up and went into the office again. He came back out with a sense of clarity. As though that one hit off a joint had cleared the cobwebs.

"Son, I'll be leaving again on Thursday, but before I go, I need a favor."

"Quit calling me son and I'll think about it."

"Now, listen to me. I need you to make a couple of runs with Raymond while I'm away."

"What kind of runs?"

"He will pick you up out front on Friday, say nine o'clock. You'll both go to a brownstone in Georgetown to drop off a gift."

"A gift?" I studied his body language. He was almost sober, except for the explosive inhale that he just took that caused sweat beads to form upon his balding head.

Whatever this little 'run' was that he was talking about, it was important. I was to dress in the clothes that he had given me.

"Make sure you look sharp," he said.

One thing I'd learned from living in D.C. for nine short months is that if you were going anywhere that involved the slightest bit of politics or business, you'd better be dressed for the part. From the visit to the Senate Dining Room to the Kennedy Center for Opera to *running gifts for coked-up lobbyists,* I needed to look my best. I even recall a gala for my great-aunt and uncle that was to raise money for my aunt's non-profit; I was in a suit with a red bowtie, and not a clip-on either. I spent the better part of two hours learning how to tie one.

Odd the kind of doors one could open by dressing well in Washington. You would think you'd need more than that. I guess it just depended on who was paying attention.

Clean shave, cufflinks, gig line, firm handshake, soft voice, eye contact, smile gently, remember the name. Those were my instructions; I had learned them at a young age.

"Such promise," I could hear family friends say. *Jesus, if they only knew.* I learned to work a room, and that wasn't the smartest thing that my family did for me. Sometimes I think about my grandma and wonder if all my 'training' was to create a better image for her and our family. That seemed more realistic.

Politics can be an uncommonly phony practice and not always a good thing for young people to witness; they need to be able to be kids for a while. I feel like a lot of my rebellion was from my family's constant worry about its image. This theory would hold true the next day, when my mom abruptly pulled me out of school.

Chapter Twenty-two

"Calvin Ducane, could you gather your things and come to my desk please."

I was already looking at Mrs. Miller, with her puffy gray hair and turquoise scarf, when she spoke those words that danced along the back of my spine.

I had known I was in trouble the moment I saw the principal's assistant, Ms. Jacobs, walk over to Mrs. Miller's desk, whisper something, and deliver a note. My stomach crumbled. I'd been in trouble countless times, but I'd never been summoned to the office in a new school where barely anyone knew me. Mrs. Miller gave no explanation. "You're wanted in the office" was all she said.

Whitman had these long hallways with artificial white lights above the checkered, linoleum floors. I was about to make the turn past the gymnasium when I took a second to think about what I would say if this pertained to my absences.

The office doors were just awful, like someone had rubbed them down with a bar of soap. There was no mistaking the woman seated on the bench right inside the door. *It was my mom. She* had these large, round sunglasses perched atop her head that gave her the nickname "The Fly" when we were growing up.

"Mom?"

"Do you have all of your things? Let's go get some lunch."

"Just tell me now if someone died."

"No one died." She grabbed her purse and stood up to leave. "We just need to discuss something…with your Uncle Jack."

And there was my answer.

We got into her Honda and sped off down River Road. She stopped at the red light at Goldsboro Road. There were a few cars ahead of us, so she turned to me and gave some thought to what she'd say next.

"Calvin, your Uncle Jack is a very busy man, so I suggest whatever it is that he has to say, you listen carefully and know that he is only looking out for your best interest."

I knew what it was. It was Gibson. Something was up, and I was involved. And now a goddamned U.S. senator is summoning me to the floor. *Holy shit.*

We turned onto Goldsboro and made the uphill drive to Massachusetts Avenue. We were well into May, and all the trees and shrubbery were blooming. There were beautiful homes and neighborhoods along Massachusetts Avenue; it made me wonder if a life like that would be possible for me one day: a loving family, a happy home, a dog, bikes in the yard. I figured quickly that I couldn't have any of those things plus be a crook, so I had decisions to make. Big decisions.

My mom didn't say much more on our way back to the Foxhall, and I remained bitter and unpleasant. I did manage to ask about lunch. "There's nothing to eat at Grandma's."

"You always say that. I'm sure we'll find something."

"That's my point. One must search for food there, unless you like Dr. Pepper, Wheat Thins, and—"

"You know, the last thing you should concern yourself with is what you're going to have for lunch."

"All right."

"Your uncle is taking time out of his day to speak to you, and I suggest you give him your undivided attention."

I could see a vein bulging on her forehead right over her big sunglasses—this was a clear sign to back off. My mom liked to use that term "undivided attention," something that had been passed down a few generations, no doubt. The only thing it told me was that I'd be sitting in the hot seat.

We made the turn into the Foxhall. The security guard was awake in the guard shack and waved us through. As we made the long drive up the winding hill toward the entrance, my mom came clean on what this lunch meeting was all about.

"Your uncle is concerned about Mr. Gibson."

"What did you tell him?"

"Nothing that he didn't already know. Trust me."

I hated whenever anyone said *trust me*. It was a curse. It always had been, and it always will be.

"Just do like I asked and be receptive," she said.

"Be receptive?"

154

"Yes, Cal. Give him your attention and apologize if you feel like you need to."

"I've got nothing to hide."

Chapter Twenty-three

So, there he sat at the head of the table, *the Honorable Senator Jack Gregory*. He was in a gray suit and navy-blue tie and had a fresh haircut. He was wearing reading glasses and was deep into the Washington Post when we arrived.

Peering over the paper, he gave out his best rehearsed greeting, "Well, hi, Calvin," he said. I could tell from his tone that he didn't really want to be there.

"Hey, Uncle Jack." He put the paper down long enough to shake hands. I usually had something witty to say, but not on that day; something was up, and I just wanted to get right down to it. By then, my grandma and my mom were seated with him at the table. I leaned up against the backside of the couch that faced the living room, cautiously keeping a distance.

"Come sit down," my mom said. I pulled back the chair closest to me and sat down. After some small talk about the weather and the church, my uncle turned his attention to me.

He tilted his head and looked at me much like a school principal would. "Calvin, do you know why your mom pulled you out of school today?"

"I do not, actually."

"Are you aware that your neighbor, this Mr. Gibson fellow, is a homosexual?"

I froze for a minute as my grandma nearly spit up her iced tea. I wanted to start laughing. I just loved how Jack Gregory could be so loose. *Tell it like it is*.

"I had a hunch."

"Well, he is, and there's nothing wrong with that, unless he has harmed you in any w—"

"He hasn't so much as laid a hand on me. Besides…." I was about to start talking like I was some hotshot, but I hesitated.

"Besides what?" my mom asked.

"I'm confident in defending myself, and it's clear to him that I don't like men."

"How do you know what you'd be defending yourself against?" my mom asked.

My uncle decided to take the floor. "Calvin, in all my years of politics, the gays have always taken a liking to me. I don't know what it is, but they have."

"If this makes you think that I'm—"

"I don't think anything. It's just that, well, Mr. Gibson is under investigation, and it's very important that you steer clear of him. You don't want to get mixed up with him, son. My guess is that his intentions are not to help you get into college."

It was then that I knew my hunch was correct. *Under investigation*. Those were beautiful words to me. I didn't know how to respond to this new twist in the story of Eli Gibson.

"So, what you're saying is, he's a gay criminal? What crime did he commit?"

"I don't have all kinds of details about him, it's a complicated matter. I'm just here to help you. You need to sever all ties with the man. It's for your own good." He drummed his fingers on the table. "You need to be investing in Calvin, not someone who doesn't have your best interest at heart."

The table went quiet. My mom was staring at me, but I refused to look at her. I was not at all surprised by the news from my uncle, but now I went from being curious about the investigation to being determined to know the whole story.

"This sure as hell is interesting," my grandma said.

"I hope you know this isn't funny," my mom said.

"You're being honest about him not acting inappropriate with you?" my uncle asked.

"Yes."

"Calvin. I realize that up until now this has been very exciting for you, the big city, the inauguration, what have you. But you've got to think about your safety, your future, your reputation, the family's reputation."

"He told me he was going to make me a millionaire." Everyone at the table seemed to squirm at this point. My uncle sat back in his chair and studied me.

"Give some thought to what we discussed here, son. I'd hate to see you get mixed up with the wrong people."

We ate lunch in silence. My grandma brought up what was happening at the church and how George Bush was already spending too much money. My uncle didn't say much. He devoured his chicken salad sandwich and was just about out the door when he turned to my mom.

"That's one sharp son of yours, Catherine. But he'll have a hard time running for president if he keeps friends like your neighbor."

My mom laughed graciously and gave him a hug. "Oh, the youngest always seems to keep life interesting."

He loved lecturing kids on what was required to run for president, leaving them either inspired or confused. On three separate occasions, Jack Gregory considered a run for the Oval Office: 1976, 1984, and 1988. I remember hearing chatter about that and reading an article in *TIME* magazine about his possible nomination. Man, I would've really been in some trouble if that had happened.

I sat back down because, in my family, there was always a follow-up, just to be sure that if it didn't sting, by God, it would now. My grandma chimed in first: "I don't know what all the fuss is about. He brought me that wonderful cake and that beautiful vase and—"

"Mother, that's not the issue here," my mother said. "The man is trying to recruit Calvin into his scheme, and I won't stand for it."

"Mom, I promise not to visit Mr. Gibson anymore," I said. "I'm not gay," I threw up the two peace signs trying to imitate Richard Nixon, "and I'm not a crook

Chapter Twenty-four

The tenth floor at Foxhall was my refuge. It was where I went to get away, to daydream, to ponder, and to smoke. I liked lighting my cigarettes like my dad did, with a book of matches. It was one of my more vivid memories of him; he would strike a match and then cup both hands, leaning down toward his chest to light a Winston. He looked cool. The matchbook also kept me from locking myself out, as the door locked automatically from the inside.

A few days after my meeting with Uncle Jack, I was home in the afternoon. It was time to head up to the roof. It was windy with a little rain; hard to light a smoke. I must've used five matches to get the damn thing lit. I finally felt the warm smoke enter my mouth, so I closed the matchbook and slipped it inside the locking mechanism.

I ambled along the gravel roof and looked out at the city, though the weather limited my view. Thoughts about where I was in my life, why I chose to involve myself with Gibson, and what to do next occupied my mind. Uncle Jack and Mom trying to end my exciting adventure was not a shock, and even though a lot of what they told me made sense, I was sure that I'd be doing some more work for Gibson in the future. Maybe Nora knew something. She had already warned me at the inauguration, and I all but ignored her.

Knowing that my uncle took time out of his busy day to inform me about Mr. Gibson's being investigated only made me more interested—maybe not the best decision on their part. Maybe if they told me that he was an accountant and that he had fudged a few numbers or something, it would've made him seem less exciting. Instead, the senator had lunch with me to explain that the man is gay and is in trouble in possibly the most powerful city in the world.

What teenager would walk away from that much excitement?

There had to be some dirt to uncover. Maybe I was being set up to take some of the heat off people. Or maybe I would find out that Gibson was being set up, and I would help him leave the country until his innocence was proven. I didn't know.

I envisioned the authorities looking for him. There would be a chase, maybe a struggle even. *Maybe a gun.* By then, I knew every corner, every hiding place and every escape there was at Foxhall, including the roof. Question was, whose side was I on?

I was looking for any excuse to stay in the game. Walking away from all the glamour, the cars, the money, and of course Nora—that just wasn't going to happen. Once I was a part of the club, I'd have everything, and at a very young age. I wasn't afraid of this guy, he never gave me the notion I was in any danger, besides the erratic driving down Pennsylvania Avenue, but that was to show off.

I skipped across the gas lines on the roof toward the door when I heard boots scratch the concrete. Just as I pulled the door open, Louis the maintenance guy had removed my matchbook.

"What's going' on, man?" he said, looking past me as though I might not be alone.

"Louis, what's up? Just came out for a smoke."

Louis had been working at Foxhall since it had opened more than twenty years ago. He was a tall, skinny Black dude with a smoky voice. He was the "Keeper of Foxhall," always snooping around, looking for things out of place.

"You know," he said, "you're not supposed to be up here."

"So I've been told. But living with a house full of women, sometimes I've got to get away."

"Don't you live with Mrs. Knutson?"

"She's my grandma."

"Oh, alright. She's a cool lady."

"You mean she doesn't drive you crazy?" She had to. Nobody gets past my grandma without a conversation.

"Ain't her I'm worried about," he said. He leaned on the stairwell railing and his eyes gave it away.

"Is this about Gibson?" I said.

"You tell me."

"Well, I'm getting lectured all over the place, so it's got to be. I'm not in any danger, and I'm not involved in anything that would hurt my family, you, Foxhall, or anybody." A mild nervousness crept up inside me. I looked down the stairwell. The feeling of people following me around was troubling.

162

"I'm just looking out, man. You never know in this town."

"You aren't kidding. But I won't make a habit of coming up here. I'll see ya around, Louis."

He caught me as I approached the door. "If you're going to run with those people, just don't do it here." It seemed to be more of an order than a request.

I let the stairwell door close and walked into the tranquil silence of the tenth floor. I could hear Louis's footsteps as he made his way down the stairwell. I wasn't in much of a hurry, so after calling for the elevator, I took another look out the window between the two large drapes. The faint sound of raindrops tapped the window. I envisioned Nora walking in the main entrance under an umbrella. Maybe I would see her soon. But I knew what that would involve.

There was no mistaking the smell inside the elevator—*Gibson was home*

Chapter Twenty-five

The elevator passed by the lobby and fell to the garage floor, allowing me to continue my way onto Mr. Gibson's residence.

I heard footsteps and keys rattling. I could hear them behind me near the boiler room door.

"What's goin' on, Calvin?" I turned around and looked up the narrow hallway. It was Louis again.

"You're all over the place, Louis."

"That's my job, man. Everything cool?" He was opening a maintenance closet and putting away a hose and bucket.

"Yeah, man, bumming around."

He started walking toward me. I turned and walked to the front of the service elevator, as though there was no harm in me using it. He got between me and the elevator.

"Didn't I tell you about using this elevator, man? This isn't for—"

"Louis, I know what it's for, but the ladies are keeping tabs on me. You going to go to bat for me or what? I'd do it for you."

"What do you mean?"

"What I mean is, if you look the other way when I'm down here, which isn't often, I'll make it worth your while.

164

I'm a little busy right now, but I'll stop by your office soon. Alright?"

"You must not have been listening upstairs."

"I was. No disrespect. This is only temporary."

He stood in front of me and hung his head. "Alright then. Just don't be making a habit of it. We've got cameras."

"I'm aware of that. But Grandma doesn't."

That was the last I saw of Louis that afternoon. The service elevator stopped at the third floor. I walked down the hallway and looked at the number on the door of his condominium: *311*. I was dressed casually: khakis with a navy-blue golf shirt and my Doc Martens, typical Washington get-around attire. I had a fresh haircut and a touch of a golfer's tan since I'd been sneaking in nine holes before work when I could. I thought about Nora and why I hadn't seen her lately.

Usually when Gibson was home, the door was left open, but not this time. I used the doorbell. I didn't hear anything inside. I just stood there. Finally, I heard the lock rattle. The door flung open and Mr. Gibson was standing there. His jaw tightened as he rubbed the back of his neck.

"How's it going?" I asked.

Without saying anything, he left the door open and walked back toward his office. He never said whether to come in or not, but I walked in and made myself at home. I immediately walked over to the wet bar to make a drink when I heard what sounded like a Shop-Vac. It was Mr. Gibson ripping a line of coke off his desk. He sat back in his chair and tilted his head. I'd never seen anyone do a line of coke with such a vengeance except in movies.

I went back to making a cocktail, this time a vodka and tonic. Fresh fruit was on the counter; perhaps he had company the night before. I used the large stainless-steel knife to cut a lime in half, then quartered it. I squeezed a wedge into my drink and took a seat in my usual leather chair.

"Have you heard much from Nora?" I asked. The long, white marks on the desk surface told me my friend had been doing coke for quite a while. I wasn't as alarmed as I should've been, but then again, I just had lunch with a U.S. senator who told me my neighbor is a criminal. Nothing was out of the ordinary anymore.

He leaned forward with a distant stare. "I'm having lunch with Nora tomorrow."

I paused and waited for an invite that didn't come. "Business lunch?"

"Why?"

I gathered from his tone that he was annoyed. "No reason."

"Ah…she's got you, doesn't she?" He leaned back and smiled. "I'm not stupid, you know."

"Nothing gets by you, Mr. Gibson." Throughout the months that I got to know him, he never asked about my sexual preference. I figured he could sniff it out if someone were gay. Considering the conversation never came up, he must've figured that I was straight. But how was he gay? He had a kid, and I'd never seen him with a partner.

166

I thought about what my Uncle Jack had told me. At the same time, I wanted to join them for lunch the next day; I needed to see if Nora.

Mr. Gibson swallowed repeatedly. It was the cocaine. It was running its course now, and he was starting to drift off. His eyes were white and sedated. He was restless in his chair. *Why, on a Thursday at happy hour, would someone get all jacked up on coke by themselves?*

"You're wondering how you can skip out on Walt Whitman and join us, aren't you?" he said, forming a grin. "A young intellect like yourself has other obligations tomorrow, no?"

"I can sign out." I got up to grab a few more ice cubes. In all my arrogance, I was already sure that I would be having lunch with the two of them the next day, so I wasn't exactly looking for his approval. And considering his current behavior, I'd most likely be driving. Thoughts of Nora in her business attire, walking into a dining room to meet us for a power lunch, as they're called. I was stirred up.

"Mind if I go look for a tie?" I asked.

He looked up from his long, drawn-out thought and glanced over at me. "As you wish," he said, his voice dry as dust.

Strolling through the suit jackets, I thought about when I had first met him and how things had changed. Back then, we talked a lot about my future, the election, West Point, and the French Riviera, none of which I knew anything about. But I was hopeful. I felt if I applied myself more in school, in the company of Mr. Gibson, my Uncle

Jack, and the people at the club, good things would fall into place. I wasn't making great marks in school, *but neither did Eisenhower, and look what he did.*

"You know, I have a shirt that fits cufflinks," I yelled into the office. He didn't hear me. I walked out into the living room and around toward the office and heard him rip another line of coke.

"Jesus."

"What was that, son?" he asked as he pinched his nostrils.

"Nothing. I said I have a shirt that fits cufflinks, but it has a stain." I was holding a pair of his cufflinks from his jewelry box. I grabbed a pair that had blue stones in the center of them. They were gold, circular cufflinks with geometric designs. They looked like miniature shields to me. Turns out they were sapphires. There must've been twenty different pairs in that mahogany jewelry box.

He wasn't listening. He had swiveled his chair around and had his feet propped up on the desk.

"I like these," I said, holding the cufflinks out in front of him. He scratched his week-old beard. I grew impatient, so I started walking out of the office to explore the closet again.

"What color is your shirt, son?"

"When you get your second wind, I'll tell you."

His dress shirts didn't have measurements on them, meaning they must've been tailored. I could hear him stumble through the living room toward the hallway that led to the closet.

He looked at a shirt I had tried on. "You clean up nice. But to get close to Nora, you need a certain something. One must blossom into that first, you see?"

"Don't be too sure, Mr. Gibson."

He laughed.

The ice in my drink had all but melted. "I'd better get going." I'm sure he didn't care if I hung around. *Maybe there was an investigation.* I wanted to drop a hint, but it didn't feel right. I'd rather hear it from Nora.

"Should I meet you here?" I said.

"That's fine. We'll dine at the Willard.

Chapter Twenty-six

Bright sun at the cloudless noon hour made the city warm and appealing. The outside of the Willard Hotel, on Pennsylvania Avenue, was originally six houses that were joined together to form the hotel in the early 1800s. Instead of demolishing them, they built around them and created what looks like a giant pop-up book. If there were ever a structure that showed its growth through the years, it was the Willard.

In typical fashion, Mr. Gibson snubbed the valet, pointing his nose higher than usual in the late spring air. We walked into the lobby where the French architecture grabbed my attention. As much as I liked snooping around the Foxhall, this place would've been a playground for me. What had to be thirty-foot pillars surrounded moon-shaped chandeliers that hung over marble floors dressed in Asian rugs and antique furniture. Small white lamps sat near each set of chairs, making it ideal for quiet conversations.

"Just look at it," he said.

The smell of fresh plants, perfume, and a hint of pipe tobacco lingered in the room. I had been a touch nervous on the drive down, but once we entered the lobby, a feeling of calm came over me. We were just two blocks from the White House, and it felt like it.

"Who knows?" Mr. Gibson said. "Maybe we'll sit next to President Bush today." He glanced at his Rolex. "Our lovely guest must be stuck in traffic. Wait here."

He walked toward the back of the lobby, which led to the dining room, and spoke to a manager in a tuxedo. I started wandering around, admiring the architecture and art, when I saw her. She tripped ever so slightly on the rug as she walked in, brushing her dark hair away from her face. A bellhop noticed and made the gesture of trying to catch her. They both laughed.

I caught her eye. She gave me a second glance as I watched her walk through the lobby.

"Hello, Nora," I said in a soft tone.

"Hello, friend," she said in her elegant voice. A peck on my cheek followed.

"I'm Eli's chaperone today," I said. "He's been on a tear lately."

"You're telling me. I showed up just to make sure he hasn't changed his name."

I carried on small talk with Nora without much effort, which was surprising, as I typically wasn't the most flattering talker with older girls.

Mr. Gibson appeared from behind me and leaned in to kiss Nora. He was really on his toes, ready to outdo me. It must've been because of our conversation the night before. It didn't make much sense to me since I was now convinced he was gay. "And how is Washington's most influential lobbyist doing today?" he said. "Not to mention its most elegant."

171

"You're never short on compliments, are you?" Nora said.

"For you? Never. Did you bring an appetite, I hope?"

"I did. I've been at it since the crack of dawn. Glad I'm done for the week."

Nora wore a tight, navy-blue suit with black hose and black stilettos. She chose a sterling silver choker necklace that rested just under her collar bone. Her hair was down and slightly curled at the bottom, giving her a look like she was ready to play all day.

She must have so many millionaires after her.

This time, Mr. Gibson wasn't his usual rude self in the dining room, most likely because of Nora, who he was apparently trying to impress for some reason. I pulled Nora's chair out for her. I think it bugged Mr. Gibson, but she was flattered.

"The *Gaya* Chardonnay," Mr. Gibson told the wine steward.

Nora looked over at him. "Did I just hear you order Gaya, Eli? You are a man after my own heart."

The waiter returned and presented the wine without Mr. Gibson interrupting. He then poured all three of us and never asked me for identification. We toasted and sipped.

Mr. Gibson put his glass down and leaned into the table. "You both need to understand something. Things will be kind of up in the air for a while. This negative press should be short lived, especially considering how inaccurate it is."

Nora glanced at me and waited for him to continue.

"My profession and my brand are under attack. Nora, you understand. Calvin plays a small role in our work, but an important one. Until you're ready to leave Washington for overseas or whatever you decide, it would behoove you to stay with us, even in a limited role."

My mind had been made up while he was speaking. "Whatever you need, sir. You all have taught me so much and have been extremely generous. I'm indebted." I couldn't have been more full of shit. I was being pulled in two directions, living a lie, and it was a slippery slope.

Nora was tight-lipped but tilted her head toward me with sincerity. I thought of our conversation on the Capitol steps and how I was not taking her advice. She hadn't been making a suggestion; it was a warning.

"Eli, it's just negative press and speculation," Nora said. "Our books are in order, and anyone, including you know who, will have a hard time proving otherwise. When you leave, just promise me you'll relax and focus on your health. You need your mind and body sharp."

You know who?

There was more talk about the next month between the two of them. They were careful not to mention too much around me. Gibson knew who my uncle was. Something about that didn't sit well with me. He was also Nora's moonlight employer, if you will, and all her smiles and charm left me feeling like I was being misled.

Chapter Twenty-seven

After a lunch of lobster and smoked salmon salad, we finished a small bottle of bubbly with crème brulee. The champagne was dry and took my buzz to a new level. It had a French label, and I enjoyed watching the waiter take such care presenting it.

"Champagne, Eli?" Nora said with concern. "Is this your two p.m. nightcap?"

"Now we're living," he said, as he watched the bubbles rise in his flute. We had three courses by now, and the table was full of glassware. The faint sound of cutlery on plates, laughter, and champagne corks made for a memorable afternoon. We took our time, though I was eager for what the rest of the day would bring.

I tried not to look at Nora, but my composure was being tested in every way. She looked sharp in her business attire. I could see her sitting in a meeting on the Hill, going over a press release or something. The world was her oyster, if she could follow the straight and narrow. Not an easy endeavor when you're mixed up with Eli Gibson.

She whispered something to Mr. Gibson, and he let out a fake laugh, then excused himself to the restroom. As soon as he left, Nora made a quick glance around and then looked at me. "Long way from Ohio, aren't you, Calvin?"

I sipped some champagne. "This is home now, so not really."

"Have you been to the Willard before?"

"Countless times," I said. "This is where I'd stay when I was a speechwriter for President Reagan."

"Cute. Do you want to go have a look around after lunch?"

Game on.

We sipped our champagne and shared some more small talk until Mr. Gibson returned. I figured he probably ripped a line of coke in the men's room. He motioned for the bill. "Can you stop by and check on Winston and such?"

"Why sure," Nora said. "Maybe I can share the responsibilities with the mayor of Foxhall, Mr. Ducane."

Mr. Gibson handed a set of keys from his suit coat to Nora. "I stocked some of your favorite ice cream, and you'll find a case of wine in the office, Pinot Noir of course."

"I suppose I should just spend the week there," she said with a sharp glance at me. She stood up and hugged Eli, and at the same time, she laid those movie-show brown eyes on me.

"Well, you two try not to get lost," Mr. Gibson said. "I'm going to visit a friend."

"Getting lost sounds like a good idea after the week I've had," she said. "Let's get you cultured, Calvin."

Nora and I walked back into the lobby. I was in love with the space when I arrived, but with a peaceful buzz and having her on my arm, I felt like I'd inherited the place.

"I'd like to freshen up," Nora said. "Wait for me." Mr. Gibson chewed on a toothpick and looked at me like we both knew something, and he wanted me to acknowledge it. I walked toward him.

"I want to thank you for lunch," I said, "but I feel like I'd be falling short."

"You're going to go far, son," he said, and just like that he was off into the city.

I watched him walk out of the lobby. I made sure to take it all in. Even if he were a crook, he showed me the city, taught me about politics, wine, cars…only one bad vice: drugs. He introduced me to authors, professors, journalists, politicians, military generals, and an intellectual, gorgeous woman named Nora Dalton. To be young and witness that much, in a city like Washington, I felt prepared for whatever stress life could muster.

Nora came up behind me and grabbed my arm, and in doing so, she grazed her body against mine, causing a cool vibration up my back. Whatever we did with the rest of our afternoon, dozing off in a warm classroom would not compare. Not even close

Chapter Twenty-eight

The gold doors of the elevator glittered when they closed. At the sound of the bell, one thing was clear—we were alone. She turned to push a button when I reached across her and pushed the number *12*, which was the top floor. There was a nervousness about her, but I think it was because she was hot and bothered, and the champagne only magnified her mood.

The elevator chimed, and we both looked up. I stood still and could see her smile from the corner of my eye. She was waiting on me. Testing me. Taunting me. Two more chimes and we were locked in a warm, gentle kiss, leaning against the wall of the elevator, my hands exploring her tight hips. She moaned and giggled and then pulled me closer, biting my bottom lip.

"Scared aren't you, Calvin?"

"Hardly."

"Meaning…."

"I knew you'd seduce me sooner or later. I've seen *The Graduate*, Miss Dalton." She laughed. All our talk was going on between hot kisses and heavy breathing. *Those eyes.*

"Well, it's our little secret."

We used the last few seconds to explore each other's bodies some more. As the elevator came to a stop, Nora brushed her hair back and pulled her skirt down.

When the doors opened, she looked both ways down the hall. "What are we doing up here anyway?"

"Wasn't this your idea?"

"Oh, you're blaming me?"

"Who knows where we're going. Let's have a look around." I poked her in the center of the back, right over the beautiful arch from her tight behind, and she walked into the hallway of the twelfth floor.

Walking aimlessly, both of us looked for somewhere to hide and continue where we had left off.

"There it is," I said. I grabbed her hand, and we hurried to the end of the hallway. A window overlooked the city and had tall drapes, much like the ones at Foxhall.

I tossed them open and pulled her inside.

She laughed. "Age is just a number, right, Calvin?" Her eyes showed a sense of temptation, like *Come and get it.*

"It certainly is today," I said.

Her hands wandered over my chest. I kissed her beneath her neck, her breath skipping as chills ran down my arms. She pulled me close and wrapped her left leg wrapped around me.

I heard something.

"Shhh," I said and held her still.

She was in no mood to stop. I wanted to peek from behind the drape, but with my luck, I'd be hauled off in cuffs. Half a minute passed, and I didn't hear anything. By this time, she had my belt undone and was not holding back. I was on the brink.

I was going to be in a lot of pain later unless we either checked in or…. "Does that stairwell lead to the roof?"

She tried the door.

Locked.

To be this close to fulfilling a fantasy, it was torture. Nora walked back and leaned into me. "Oh, Calvin."

"The way I see it, we might as well wait. We're only going to do this once, so we might as well make it count."

"Make it count?"

"Yeah. The full experience. No sophomore year stuff."

A bright, eager smile came over her face. "I guess we'll push this back 'til Friday."

"I'll be ready."

"I noticed," she said. We walked down the hall, her arm looped through mine. We kissed in the elevator again, though we regained our composure as we prepared to step off.

"Friday will be fun," I said

Her demeanor changed the moment we entered the lobby. "I agree Calvin."

I understood. She had to maintain her public image, just in case she ran into someone. I walked her outside to her cab, where she offered me a professional handshake. Flags whipped in the wind on that warm, late-spring afternoon. I watched the yellow cab drive off, wondering where she was headed and who she would encounter. I tried to envision the coming Friday night on the crowded train back to Embassy Row.

***

"This is the red line to Shady Grove," the voice said over the speakers. The train felt like it was being sucked into the Pennsylvania Avenue Metro stop. The sound of iron on iron scraping the tracks and the quick acceleration and flashes of light from the tunnel made my mind spin, like I was escaping something. I had only four more stops and I'd be at Friendship Heights, where I'd catch the bus to Mass Avenue and then mosey down the street to Foxhall.

I noticed a man in a plain suit with broad shoulders and slicked back hair. Though he wore shades, I could swear he stared at me for a moment. At the next stop, I noticed that he moved a couple of seats closer to me and checked me out yet again. I made a mental note of his face and exited the train. I looked back but didn't see him. All I needed was a jealous boyfriend tailing me. Or worse, someone from my uncle's camp keeping tabs on me. With Mr. Gibson leaving town, and Nora and I planning an evening together, there was no way it could all just fall into place without an implosion of sorts. Not with my luck.

The bus's diesel engine roared off and left me dodging fumes as I began the walk to Foxhall. Traffic buzzed up and down Mass Avenue, beneath the last of the afternoon sunlight, when a set of eyes locked on me. A quick tie of the shoe allowed me to see the red Cadillac that slowed down right behind me. The man from the train, with his slicked back hair and black shades, slid into the passenger's seat, and the car sped away.

I continued walking down Mass Avenue past Foxhall, and once it was clear, I crossed the street and lit a smoke. The possibilities of who they could be kept my mind busy. I instantly ruled out Nora's involvement. She had my best interest in mind. The question I had was, assuming he and the driver were somehow connected with Gibson, were they friend or foe? I'd say trailing me around Washington answered that question.

But, they knew who I was now, and they knew where I lived.

Chapter Twenty-nine

As anxious as I'd been all day about meeting Nora, I was ready to have some serious fun. A long, deep breath in front of the hallway mirror helped. That was the halfway point to Gibson's condo. I looked all right in blue jeans, a white button down, and a sport coat. As usual, I wore my wing tips, which seemed too dressy for blue jeans, but I thought of them as my lucky shoes. I passed on a haircut because it would make me look boyish. I wanted Nora to spend her evening with the guy she remembered from the parties and the hotel.

Since I was as welcome there as anyone, I checked the door instead of knocking, and it was unlocked. My nervousness came back for a second, as I didn't know what I'd find inside.

Mr. Gibson's dog Winston ran over and greeted me with a wagging tail.

"Hey, little guy." Winston ran back to the living room and jumped up on the couch. I followed him over and sat with him for a minute, scratching his ears.

No one was home. I looked in the office on my way to the kitchen: nobody. There was a clue in the kitchen: a case of wine, with a couple bottles missing, sat on the counter. It was a chardonnay from California—*Cakebread*. A yellow sticky note was on the counter in front of the wine.

Cal, too early to start drinking?
Chard in fridge, so delish!
Ran to store
See you soon, N

She drew a heart next to her name. As I read the note, my stomach churned. There were two wine glasses on the granite countertop, one with a small touch of wine in it and lipstick on the rim. The bottles in the fridge were still warm, so I'd just missed her. I poured a half glass and walked into the living room where Winston and I bonded. The light from the evening sun found its way into the wine glass, causing a crystal glow on the coffee table. The wall-length mirror behind me made everything so bright with the sunlight, I could barely make out what was across the room.

My tracks were covered for the night. As far as my mom knew, I was going to a reggae concert in Georgetown and then crashing at Roshan's. She bought it. Turns out, a few friends were doing just that, but my plans were different. I stood up and looked at myself in the mirror. I felt good about my appearance, though I didn't know what to say when Nora arrived. I needed something witty, so I sat back down and took a few sips of wine.

The front door opened, and I heard a grocery bad tear. "Aww, shoot," Nora said. I jumped out of my seat to help. A loaf of French bread and some other items had hit the floor.

"That was some entrance, Dalton."

"Just like they taught me in charm school."

Her perfume again. She knew what she was doing. I took one of the bags out of her hands and checked out what she was wearing, determining how easily I could take it off. She was probably still dressed from being downtown. She wore a black skirt, cut just above the knee. Her top was a thin, pearl-colored blazer with a low-cut halter top of the same color, barely exposing her chest. The skirt had a large silver buckle that looked like it might be tough to navigate.

"Aren't you a lifesaver," she said.

I led her into the kitchen. "Just an innocent bystander."

"That damn bag started tearing in the elevator. My luck lately."

She kicked off her black stilettos, and I felt that buzz in my midsection again. I placed the grocery bag on the counter while she poured some wine. She sipped and motioned to fill mine as well. I grabbed the bottle, poured some into my glass, and then blocked her into the corner of the granite countertop.

"Mr. Ducane, what *are* you doing?" she said innocently. I backed away, as if only teasing. Nora Dalton wasn't about to just jump in the sack like we were in her parents' basement.

"Wait," I whispered. "You hear that?"

"I don't hear anything." She sipped her wine again. "Exactly. Nice, isn't it?"

I was about to make my move, but I paused. It was too soon. Not yet.

184

"Why don't you take Winston for a walk, and I'll start dinner," Nora said. "You a fan of salmon, Calvin?"

"Never had it."

"I think you'll like it." She took another sip of wine and smiled. "Promise."

Chapter Thirty

Back from a quick walk with Winston, I turned on some jazz that I'd never heard of before from Mr. Gibson's CD collection. I walked past the kitchen a few times, admiring Nora. I would keep my eyes on her until she would notice and look over at me—then I'd look away. She would laugh quietly as she tasted her cooking, telling me she knew what I was up to. I didn't care. I had been a risktaker at an early age, and this was the biggest risk of my life so far.

The fish was sautéed and then broiled with fresh garlic, butter, and lemon. She served it with broccoli and roasted redskins. After dinner, we wound up on the couch for more wine. We had switched to red, a pinot noir from Oregon named *Ponzi*.

"This is the best I've ever had," I said.

"You'd think it's from France." She gave the bottle a look in front of the chandelier. "Cool name too."

I had a hard time relaxing. I wasn't sure why, but Gibson's presence was in the room. I almost wished we were at her place, like she had suggested earlier in the week. His condo would never be the same to me if she and I spent the night together, but I was willing to live with it.

As the music continued, we picked up where we had left off at the Willard Hotel. She straddled me on the couch and began kissing along my neck. "

You know, sometimes—"

"Sometimes what, Cal?"

We continued to explore each other. "Sometimes a person comes into your life…."

"Mmmhmm."

"And it's like you're both experiencing a rite of passage, you know?"

I expected some sort of response, instead she just moaned softly collapsed into me. I guided her down on the couch and helped her out of her blouse. I remembered the sleepless nights and daydreaming about her in school, and I let it all pull me toward her half-naked body.

The sound of her breathing told me we were ready for the bedroom. We began our move. I noticed her look behind the couch into the mirror, which I found odd. Standing behind her, I ran my arms around her waist. I looked in the mirror at her and felt our chemistry slip a little.

"You all right?" I said.

"Ever play rough, Calvin?"

Startled, I tried to keep the momentum going. "Not like I want to."

She slapped me. "Take me right here."

I gazed into those eyes I've adored since the first moment I saw them. They were darker now, desperate.

She slapped me again.

There were risks involved in this life with Gibson, risks in leading a double life, in being exposed, but sleeping with Nora made it all worthwhile.

I shoved her toward the hallway. "That what you want?" She showed more and more arousal, running her hands along her chest and neck.

I should've been afraid of her by now, after all, she was protected. Gibson had his muscle, and they were not gentlemen. For all I knew, they had already taken people out. "No backing out now." I pushed her again toward the guest room.

"I guess you can't give it the old college try, can you, Cal?" She stood by the door and waited for me. When I got close, she dug her nails in my chest and bit my chin. Although I'd never experienced any uninhibited, rough sex, I sensed her desire. I stood still, watching her. She pulled me into the room and reached for my belt.

"Got big plans for us?" I said. She flipped on a small lamp so I could see her get undressed.

She stood before me naked, and I took a mental snapshot. I knew what it was she wanted. I kicked the door closed. "Nowhere to run now, Nora."

She walked over to me and dropped to her knees. Stripping me of my clothes, she pulled me in front of a full-length mirror and kept her eyes on me the whole time.

Nora folded my belt in half and handed it to me. "This better hurt."

***

In the guest room, with the red lamp and tall candles on the dresser, Nora took me to a place I'd never been. I watched us in the mirror. Some of it was passionate, some purely physical, and some was downright angry. After our long bout of pent-up sexual aggression, never to be repeated, I wasn't experiencing the typical after-sex relaxation. I was nervous, and it was time for her to explain what was going on. This was no ordinary affair. But before I could say anything, she wrapped herself in a sheet and got up to leave the room. I scrambled to my feet and extended my arm across the doorframe.

"Pardon me, Romeo."

"I need to know something," I said. "Tell me why."

She laughed. First out loud, then into her hands as she slipped along the wall and down to the floor, where she sat laughing. I sat on the bed and watched her. She was coming down from our adventure, shaking slightly. The night had taken its toll on her. And on me.

I got up and tried to make the room right, minus the broken lamp and some tangled drapery. Winston had been waiting outside the door and followed me into the kitchen.

Not two minutes later, Nora was standing in front of the couch, putting on her earrings and buttoning her blouse.

"I just remembered I left some work on my desk," she said. "I've got to run." Her tone wasn't cold, but it wasn't sincere either. It was just an abrupt departure, and one that left me feeling inadequate, like I came up short or something. Her eye makeup was smudged, and there were marks on her neck and cheekbone that gave me a flashback to how rough we had been. I couldn't understand why she would leave. I was sensing an all-night affair, and now she's got one foot out the door.

"What's the matter?"

She stumbled with one of her shoes and looked at me. "Nothing, just have to run."

"About earlier…that almost got out of hand, huh?" *It did get out of hand.* She stood in the foyer, listening to me. "A bit out of the ordinary for a Midwestern boy, you know?"

"You sure fooled me, Calvin."

And then the door closed behind her

Chapter Thirty-one

I had not heard from Nora all week. I had a hunch this would happen. *Maybe she's busy with work. Maybe she's out of town.*

Roshan and I planned to play golf on the following Monday. I looked forward to trying to empty my mind for a while—and empty his wallet. It only took ten minutes for him to start asking about Nora and Gibson.

"You can't repeat any of this, you know?" I said.

Roshan exhaled his smoke and just smiled. He was seated next to me in a Congressional golf car. We had just grabbed drinks at the turn and were about to approach the tenth tee box. "Squire, I couldn't care less."

"Then why are you asking?"

"I don't know. Kill some time."

"Well, you'll care after I tell you this " The school year had ended, and we looked forward to enjoying our employee perks. "The whole week, I'm thinking it's not even going to happen. Any guy our age would think the same. If you saw her, you'd agree. I wish I had a picture."

"I wish you did too." He swung at his ball, and it faded into the creek. "Shit."

"So, we meet at this guy's condo. The one that's two floors up from my grandma's. She cooks up this incredible dinner. Wine, jazz music, she's out of her shoes." I hit my shot into a sand trap, and we walk back to the cart.

"Did your mom and grandma know you were—"

"Hell no. Anyway, we moved to the couch. More wine, more jazz."

"Yeah?"

"I still couldn't believe it, but things kept going. She's straddling me on the couch. Getting kinky." I paused and looked over at him. "Then, it gets weird. She starts getting downright evil. I'm not kidding."

"Evil?"

With a hand on the wheel of the cart, I lean over. "Then she says, *Take me right here.*"

"No."

"She starts clawing at me, throwing blows, biting, just flat out begging for it. I didn't know what to do, but I was at full attention, if you know what I mean."

"Don't tell me you balked."

"I surprised myself, that's what I did."

"Huh?"

"I pushed her into the spare room and started taunting her. She loved it, couldn't get enough. I thought we were breaking the law, I'm not kidding."

"Well, she's a hooker, right?"

"No, she's not a goddamned hooker," I said, my face heating like a stove coil. "Where did you get that idea?"

"Easy there, Squire. I thought you said the guy she worked for had prostitutes."

"She's his bookkeeper and arranges other business for him. She's one of the most elegant, classy, gorgeous women I've ever encountered, and she takes her sex on the rare side." I stepped out of the golf cart. "His *hookers*, as you call them, are mostly men anyway. Young men, I might add."

"Young men?" Roshan said. "You're a young man."

"Don't even think about it, Rosh. If that were the case, I'd have punched my way out by now." I thought of Nora. *Why did she leave so abruptly? What did I do wrong?*

"I've got to see this chick," he said.

"Well, that's the strange part. I want to see her too. But once we were done, she was gone."

"Uh-oh."

I walked to my ball and replayed the night in my head. That wasn't a young couple laughing and making love. That was two people fighting the evil out of their systems through sexual deviance. I would never look at sex the same again, and the whole thing left me shaken.

We walked up to the green. "I know it's only Monday," I said. "That's what, ten days? If I don't hear back by Wednesday, I need to go find her. I'm sick of dropping quarters in the payphone."

"What's her name?"

I looked at him. "I'll tell you, but you can't repeat it to anyone."

"Fair enough," he said.

I pictured her face. "Nora Dalton."

I loved to say her name.

I loved her.

***

Depending on the weather, Nora did her running either in Rock Creek Park or on the National Mall. During inclement weather, she would run the Mall, as it was closer to a Metro stop. On that warm Friday morning in late June, the skies were clear besides a few cotton ball clouds hanging over the city.

I decided I'd go for a run on the Mall.

While riding the Metro to the Smithsonian station, I closed my eyes and attempted to get my thoughts together. *What if she's there? What if she doesn't want to see you? If you got used and thrown out with the trash, then you'll need to accept that. Don't try to turn this into something it's not.*

I stretched near the Washington Monument and watched tourists take photographs and react to the architecture. I decided to run east to Fourth Street and loop around and run past the Reflecting Pool and up to the Lincoln Memorial. I had a deflated feeling that she wouldn't be there. For all I knew, she had left town with Mr. Gibson or someone else from his entourage. I had grown jealous.

I approached the Washington Monument again. A memory came to mind of how, during a visit as a boy, I would stand flush up against the monument and stare straight up until it made me dizzy. *Now look at me.* The Lincoln Memorial was on the western end of the Reflecting Pool, almost a mile away. I decided to walk the remaining distance to enjoy the beauty.

My plan was interrupted, however, when I noticed the unmistakable shape of a woman in the glistening morning sunlight. She was running along at a good clip and had just passed the steps of the Lincoln. A spark of heat ran through my body as I sprinted along the Reflecting Pool. I became anxious trying to think of something to say if it were her. Nothing too friendly, that would be phony. *Don't worry, I walked Winston.* Or *You know, we still have a case of wine to drink.* No. I lost sight of her. I picked up the pace. Rounding the granite and marble landmark, I slowed down on the gravel and looked toward the Potomac.

From the east, the sun reflected off the river. A rowing team approached, heading north and sculling in unison. As the boat passed my vision, I saw her. She was stretching out and facing the river. Thoughts of our Friday night together were alive and well in my head.

"You up for another mile or two?" I said.

She jumped back and looked in my direction. I stared ahead at the river. The sun blinded her, but she knew it was me.

"Calvin," she said, "you have to leave me alone."

A sudden frost entered my veins. "What do you mean? Why?"

Sweat beads formed at the base of her chin and dripped off. Her gray *College of William & Mary* T-shirt showed the signs of a long run. She looked all around, but not necessarily for another person.

She pushed me out of her way. "Calvin, go!"

"Is everything alright?" She started to run away. I stood still. *This isn't happening.*

I caught up to her on the opposite side of the Lincoln Memorial. She had slowed to a walk, and I got closer to her so as not to yell.

"Nothing is alright," she said. "That's why you haven't heard from me. You thought you might whisk me off somewhere? Well, you're wrong. You need to just go away."

"What's going on? There's more to it, isn't there?" She made a point of not looking at me. "Isn't there, Nora?" She walked away, the gravel kicking up dust under her shoes.

Using her shirt, she wiped sweat away from her face, "You need to get lost."

"But why? What did I do? I thought—"

"You're not cut out for this."

"Why do you keep saying that? Just come with it."

She looked in my eyes. "Do you remember at the inauguration when I said you needed to leave, to get out?"

"I remember."

"You should've listened to me." She walked toward the monument. I remembered that we had spoken about my uncle and that Gibson might be under investigation.

"What the hell does that have to do with us?" I looked at the ground, and a knot tightened in my stomach. "I thought we had something."

She got up close to me and spoke in a whisper, "Calvin, a callboy from a boys' home was brought to Washington with a group. He wasn't part of a blackmail sting, he was brought here to service someone. Broke and strung out on drugs, he started making threats. They silenced him." She scanned the area and continued. "They, meaning shadow government people, do you know what I mean by that? They're not elected, but they're powerful. No one can get to them."

"I'm supposed to believe that? Sounds more like a scare tactic to chase me away."

"Suit yourself. I'm leaving, and you're not welcome to come with. It's got to be this way." Nora's pained expression was one I'd never seen before. She always carried herself so confidently. Something in her lifestyle and her choices was beginning to take its toll on her. I watched her as she tugged at her shoelaces and then took off down the path next to the Reflecting Pool.

It's got to be this way. Those were her final words to me, the words I'd have to live with unless I could convince her otherwise. She continued running, not looking back. She ran with such grace. The knot in my stomach turned to nausea. My heartbeat picked up, and my legs became weak, as though I might fall.

It's got to be this way.

***

"Nora, wait. Hear me out." I caught her boarding the train at the Constitution Avenue station. I got in just as the doors were closing. She turned around and grabbed my arms. She looked around with caution as the train left the station. "Move to the back." I did as she said and already had in mind that I would be honest. I would tell her that her final words would haunt me for the rest of my life if we ended it.

I held onto the railing over her head as the train began swaying. "Did I do something? Or not do something?" Words were becoming more difficult to find. "I realize that you're in a different part of your life, but, 'It's got to be this way.' Why did you say that? Why—"

"Because you're one of his pawns, Calvin! You're a blackmail pawn. And I could be killed just telling you that. "

"What are you saying? That makes no sense. Why would he want to blackmail me?"

"It's not about you. He wants your uncle."

I stood motionless. *My Uncle Jack.* And if there were photos—or worse, a tape of us—what would happen to my family?

The train stopped at a station and Nora had her eyes closed. She held onto one of the overhead handles while the train swayed to a stop so another could clear the station. She was elsewhere, probably home in Virginia, far away from all the greed and filth of Washington.

"Nora, my Uncle Jack is an honorable man. He's a Marine. And my Aunt Emma…no. This isn't happening. If Gibson somehow threatened to use me to bait my uncle, I would be disowned and left for dead. That, I can assure you. You can't let him do this."

She turned to hide the tears. "The plan was to see if you were experienced."

"Experienced at what?"

198

"Pretty much what you're thinking. It sounds like an odd practice, but that's how he recruits young men, and women for that matter. If I tell him no, then he holds incriminating evidence over me."

"He blackmails you."

"Well, look who's catching on." Nora looked behind her and stood closer to me. "He *threatens* to blackmail me. He's never had to because I always comply."

It was never my intention to learn what she was telling me—or maybe I didn't want to. I doubted Nora was a prostitute. *Fucking is for amateurs. I forgot who said that.*

"And he threatens you?"

"He has ways of getting what he wants." She pulled me toward her, and we sat down on the bench that emptied at the back of the train. *If only we were headed somewhere; somewhere far away and safe like the Blue Ridge Mountains, maybe the coast. If only—*

Nora curled her hand around my arm and laid her head on my shoulder. I could feel the vibration of the train coming through her warm body as we swayed together in unison. I enjoyed the moment. I wanted it to last, maybe find our way back to her place. Too bad.

"And his goal was to videotape us in some cult-like sex ritual and then…use the tape as a tool for blackmail?"

"That's just it, Calvin." She waited until she had my full attention. "He already did."

ACT III

Chapter Thirty-two

"Nor thieves, nor covetous, nor drunkards, nor revilers, nor
extortioners shall inherit the kingdom of God."
— 1 Corinthians 6:10

"Was he in the room?"

"Who?" Nora said.

"Nora, please. I can read between the lines." We had gotten off the Metro and ducked into the Old Ebbitt Grill to talk.

"First, you need to calm down."

"Calm down?" Easy for you to say. All you did was make another random sex tape, which you're probably going to get paid for."

"You have no right to say that, Calvin. Give me a chance to explain."

Dark wood and soft lighting created a posh atmosphere, but I couldn't appreciate it with everything that was on my mind. We ordered sparkling water and salads and sat in the quiet. Nora looked away from me and said, "I didn't have a choice. I don't do those types of *favors,* as Eli calls them, but one time I did, and he's used it against me for four years now."

The thought of her being coerced like that by Gibson made me want to kill him. He had to be breaking some federal or state sex trafficking law, but what did I know. The server delivered our salads and fresh bread. The food looked great, but I didn't feel like eating. Sitting back in the leather booth, I watched as the bartender wiped down bottles on the shelves behind him. "And he thinks he'll get money out of Uncle Jack?"

"He hasn't said. His cards are close to the vest."

"The people I've met at the dinners and parties, the inauguration—has he ever pulled this stunt on any of them?"

Nora was careful with her words. I felt like she was holding back, not being completely revealing, as if she were under strict orders from Eli. "There's no need to discuss that right now."

"Really? And when would be a good time? After my family has disowned me?"

"Calvin, please." Her shoulders slumped. She looked young and pissed off—like a college coed who had just flunked an exam. "I need you to be patient while I try to figure something out."

"Oh, I see. So, now my fate rests in the hands of the token woman, who blackmailed me for some sleaze ball lobbyist. Yeah, this should end well."

"Fuck you, Calvin."

Nora wasn't telling me much. Her answers were vague, and then she would pause and try to figure out what not to say. I was no longer infatuated with her. I felt like we were on different teams now. She was looking out for Eli, and I was looking out for a ticking timebomb in the form of a sex tape.

"And here I thought Virginia girls were proper," I said.

"Give it time, and I'll speak to Eli."

"You know we're stuck in this together."

"Looks like it."

***

An ache formed in my chest, like a hot knife had been thrust into my ribcage. It's been said that anger is only one letter away from danger. Not only did I believe that—the thought of violence toward Eli Gibson was very much on the table.

The Foxhall had security, cameras and all, but ever since being blackmailed by Mr. Gibson and Nora, I didn't feel safe. I slept with a knife under my pillow and a golf club within arm's reach. The typical sounds of the Massachusetts Avenue traffic used to be comforting, but now I lie awake, listening and waiting for something, someone to crawl over the railing to come take me away. But why? If the first part of my blackmail was complete, why would anyone, Gibson included, want me dead or missing? They hadn't even extorted anyone yet, but that didn't keep me from being paranoid.

I woke up out of a dream in a cold sweat. The scene was of a messenger in the Dirksen Senate Building standing outside my uncle's office. *Delivery for Senator Gregory, delivery for Senator Gregory!* Like something out of a low-budget, black-and-white film. Then the building catches on fire.

From my days of mischief and rebellion in Ohio, the patterns of disconnect returned. Work, friends, family life, I pushed it all away. The willingness to right the ship was there, but I needed to keep my eye on the horizon or I'd lose that rabbit for sure.

Walking into work, I grabbed *The Washington Times* off the desk. On the front page was a sizable column dedicated to none other than Eli Gibson: "*WHITE HOUSE PROBE CONTINUES*." The valet manager, Dan, walked into the office and noticed me.

"Everything cool, Calvin?"

"What's that? Oh, yeah. Tired. Got to start sleeping better."

Dan looked behind us and then shut the office door. "Gibson keeping you out late?" He wasn't smiling.

"Where'd you get that idea?"

"I used to do some side jobs for Gibson. Then it got a little…weird."

"Oh, it's weird all right," I said. "So, you've seen today's paper?"

"Question is, has your uncle seen it?" Dan took the newspaper from my hands and scrolled through the article again.

"My uncle?"

"Yeah. Your uncle. Jack Gregory. Democratic Senator from South Carolina."

"I don't remember telling you about my uncle before. How did you know that?"

He handed the newspaper back to me, "Listen, if you're going to keep running with Gibson, you're not going to work here. Please don't take it as any kind of threat, just take it for what it is."

That news didn't come as a surprise. I was sure there would be more fallout like that from others going forward.

I sat back down on the wooden bench in the valet office and finished reading the article.

Eli J. Gibson, Republican lobbyist to many Washington elites, is under investigation for blackmail, prostitution, credit card fraud, and other charges. Known for throwing lavish parties at his home in the Kalorama neighborhood of Northwest Washington, Gibson allegedly connected his clients with sexual services. Expensive male and female escorts, many of them minors, were allegedly flown in from various parts of the country to play a part in his blackmailing schemes. Mr. Gibson has been unavailable for questioning.

My hunch about him wasn't even close, it was worse. I remember standing outside of my grandma's condo, putting golf balls on the green patio carpet, telling myself I'd come too far to turn back.

I needed to discover how deeply entrenched Mr. Gibson was in this corruption. I needed to discover the truth. It was the wrong thing to do, and I knew that. The desire to know meant everything to me, and I couldn't explain why. I just needed to know.

***

During a long night of sprinting for cars and being grateful for dollar-bill tips, I had a chance to do some thinking. For starters, I missed just being a kid, being a valet, and playing golf on Mondays. Life was exciting when I first landed in Washington. Exciting, but simple. And here I was, nearly a year later, leading two lives and refusing to walk away. The question I had for myself was, how do I go from the new kid at school with a cool job to a courier for a political blackmailer? In my youth, most of the trouble I caused was the kind I could walk away from. Maybe a slap on the wrist. And now I'm risking having my picture in the *Washington Times* for crimes that I didn't even commit.

It probably would've served me well if I didn't have so much time to think. I wasn't sure what to do next. Where to stay. Who to trust. My life was now being run on one of two emotions: paranoia or fatigue. Something had to give, and my intuition said it wasn't going to be me.

I thought long and hard about trying to track down Nora again. Unless she had constant security, which didn't seem likely, I could find time to see what she'd come up with since our last meeting. For my own security, we would need to be out in public. My objectives needed to be clear and precise. I needed to grow up in a hurry because she was out of my league, not to mention very busy. And if we were going to be in this venture together, I needed to build some form of trust with her. She would most likely be at work the following day. I decided I would head downtown to pay her a friendly visit.

Chapter Thirty-three

The water was cold in the marble sink of Nora's office building. I splashed it on my face. I thought of what I would say. I wiped my face clean, leaving a little water on my hands to run through my hair. I took some deep breaths and walked out of the men's room. Thinking about Nora always got me excited, but this time was different. Thoughts of her scent, like fresh berries and sandalwood, and her infectious laugh would have to wait until I could look into her eyes as she answered my questions. This is, after all, the same woman who weeks before had given me the sex of my life, and then tried to blackmail me and maybe worse.

What kind of woman takes a young guy for a ride like that, has Viking sex with him, promises him more and more, and then surprises him with a nightmare? *I know what kind of woman.*

Moments later, she appeared from the elevators with two men in dark suits. I was still a distance from them. I caught her eye. The look of panic took over her otherwise pleasant, attractive face. She shook me off with her head and began walking toward the main entrance with the suits. Not knowing what to do, I walked to the elevator. It opened immediately, and I could smell her scent for real this time. I put my back to the wall, hoping I would catch a glimpse from her. She stared right at me as the doors closed. She was near the exit, speaking with the elder of the two men and pulling her dark hair behind her ear. She discreetly gave me the sign of *one minute*. I took the elevator to the second floor and immediately came back down.

Nothing.

I left the building and walked out front, stalling some more, looking both ways down the block. The way she had looked at me when the elevator doors were closing made me feel that she had something to say. She'd better.

I was desperate. I needed her to come clean and perhaps get my name out of the investigation. Considering our conversation on the Mall, she had to know more about what was happening than she had led me to believe. There was little chance of taking down a powerful, corrupt lobbyist who's protected by former Secret Service, but with Nora's help, maybe.

I looked in the lobby one more time, causing the security guard to turn and give me a stare. Nora was gone. *So close.* Maybe I would get another chance. Outside, there was a stone bench, just off the sidewalk. I took a seat and pulled the *Times* out of my backpack and continued reading. The article painted an ugly picture: homosexual prostitution ring discovered being run by prominent power broker, Eli Gibson. It went on to say how he had repeatedly arranged late-night tours of the White House and had Secret Service agents who moonlighted as his bodyguards. "Raymond and Phillip," I said under my breath.

The brakes of a car skidded to a halt on the pavement in front of me. I lowered the paper. The back door of a D.C. cab opened.

There was no mistaking the legs.

"Get in."

"Just like that?" I said.

"Just like that."

"Why the hell would I trust anything you say?"

"Just c'mon." Rain began to fall. I flung my backpack over my shoulder and got into the cab.

The driver took off even before I could close the door. Nora crossed her legs and sat away from me, almost guarded. She was very confident, not like the emotional mess I had left in the train station.

"Interesting day?" I said.

"Chaotic."

"Who were the suits?"

Nora looked at me while she thought up a lie. "Couple of consultants in town for a convention."

"Like a surveillance convention? One-way mirrors, video cameras?"

"You really should consider yourself lucky, Calvin."

"I thought I was when I had you."

The cab driver stole a quick glance at me in the rearview mirror.

Nora said, "Not all of Eli's talent has it as good as you do."

"Talent? That's hilarious." My hands began to shake. I thought for a moment about what she had said. She wanted to see if maybe I could be bought. Take an eighteen-year-old kid, give him all the sex and booze and drugs he could want, and he'll do whatever you tell him, right? So far, that's what was happening.

"You know everything?"

"About?"

I worried about the cab driver. "Today's newspaper."

"Oh, that." She pulled out her lipstick and applied some using a pocket mirror. "I'm afraid I know too much."

Neither of us spoke for a while. The cab took a sharp left turn, leaving us staring at the U.S. Capitol building. Even in the steady rain, it was majestic and powerful. The driver cut someone off heading into another traffic circle and said something in an Eastern European language when they honked at him. Nora slipped her shoes off and curled her feet up onto the seat.

"There's something I need to tell you," I said. "A few things, actually."

She out the cab window. "Likewise."

"First, where are we headed?"

"We can start at my place. I have some work to do, and a glass of wine sounds good."

I leaned back in my seat and let my imagination take over for a moment. *I'm going to her place.* No matter what happened to Eli Gibson, I was going to get a closer look at her life that day. Never mind that I might get strapped to a chair and beaten by shady bodyguards, I had a chance to find out what was really going on with her and Gibson and where I stood in the mix.

"Where do you live?"

"Arlington."

"No bodyguards, no weirdos?"

"Haven't we seen enough?"

The driver dropped us off in front of her townhouse in Arlington, a suburb of D.C. on the Virginia side. It was modest, with sandstone and light pink brick along the facade. A small porch with room for two chairs sat out front, and blooming bushes and small flowers dotted the landscaped yard. I thought again about what might happen inside, and I told myself that if anything were a little off, I was out of there. *Look for mirrors*. I wasn't afraid, but I was, at the very least, prudent. *And no sex*. That was a hard one. Nora was likely as much of a victim as I was with Gibson, but I couldn't be too certain.

The raindrops were the size of dimes when we stepped out of the cab. She grabbed my hand and pulled me away from the house. "C'mon," she said. We ran for a moment in the rain. There was a small, roof-covered structure nearby that held the mailboxes. The rain soaked us as we ran. Her hair was matted down, and she gave me a long stare, allowing those eyes to go to work on me.

"No luck," she said. She grabbed her mail and took one more look into her mailbox.

"Expecting something?" I thought of Gibson and the blackmail tapes.

"Yes and no. I'll explain when we get inside. It's nothing that has me worried."

I wiped the rain from my face. "I wish I could say the same, but I'm basically being blackmailed, and you knowingly played a part in it."

She leaned against the mailboxes and looked back at me, the raindrops on her face only enhancing her beauty. "How old are you again, Calvin?"

"I'm legal, if that's what you're asking. But no matter my age, I have a family's image to protect, let alone the reputation of a U.S. senator."

She thought for a moment and then began a slow jog back to her townhouse.

We got inside, and she slipped out of her shoes. There was a great room with a fireplace just adjacent to the foyer and a kitchen with a wet bar. From the refrigerator, she pulled out a bottle of chardonnay and reached for two glasses.

"Calvin, if you're worried about my honesty, I understand. But things have changed. I was sucked into this just like you. I was promised a lot. A lot that I didn't care about. Eli swindled me, he blackmailed me, and before I knew it, he used me to lure people his way. I was like a liaison, and not in a good way. You may be thinking that I'm one of his call girls, but that's not the case."

"And I'm the courier," I said. "He's more than just a blackmailer, and you know it. If you deny it and pretend this is all going to go away, you're only going to hurt yourself. He's going to disappear and leave people like you, me, and

Philip to take the fall." We took a seat in the great room. "So, what were you expecting in the mail?"

She looked out the window and let out a long breath. "Okay, bear with me here. Over the years, Eli has run up many, many credit cards. Some real, some fake. I noticed it by mistake one time when I saw a receipt from a manual machine, and I didn't recognize the person, but I recognized the handwriting."

"Eli's."

"As part of my duties, I'm trying to gather up the paper trail with the help of someone in the credit card business. It's a long shot, but he's pretty much stuck, which means I'm stuck."

"I think that list would be much longer than Eli and yourself, no?"

"Time will tell," she said.

"What other trails are in need of gathering?"

"Calvin, I'm not going to lay out the inventory for you. Your role will be to do as your told, and some of that will entail nothing at all. Are we clear?"

She sure was bossy when she needed to be. "It's more curiosity than anything. I'm—"

"I don't give a damn, Calvin. I need your head in the game. This is some serious shit we're dealing with."

Her losing her patience with me after that dirty con at Foxhall took some nerve, but according to her, she didn't have a choice. It was looking like I was out of choices too.

"We need his ledger," Nora said. "It has tremendous value to Eli. Catch my drift?"

"So, if we can somehow get the ledger, we can use it?"

"The boat already left, but keep swimming, you're almost there."

"Well, I think I have a plan, but it needs to happen quick."

"Oh!" She flashed a nervous smile at me. "You have an elaborate plan to get us out of a White House probe, Calvin? You're going to outdo the FBI? Are you an undercover CIA agent? Oh, that's right, you're in high school. Maybe the debate team is going to come riding in on white horses to save the day."

"We're breaking into the Kalorama house tonight."

She laughed. "And what are you going to accomplish there, MacGyver?"

"That's what I need from you. What am I looking for in there besides the ledger? Video equipment? More credit card evidence? Whatever it is, it needs to be destroyed."

"Calvin, there are clues and evidence for days at Kalorama. Going in and swiping records, ledgers, videos, it won't make much of a difference. And besides, I don't know that you're up to the job."

"We can't wait. It has to go down tonight."

Nora stood up and looked out the front window. "Well, then I guess we better get going."

Chapter Thirty-four

"I'd better drive," I said. Nora and I were outside her condo, leaving for Kalorama.

"Does it matter?"

"In case things get hairy, I want to be at the wheel."

"I feel safer already."

We drove down Macomb Avenue and circled the neighborhood. "We'll drive by and then head over to Mitchell Park and walk back. The garage door in back should be easy to get into. The trees will provide cover, but we'll have to be quiet." I thought about my adventures snooping around Foxhall and how quiet I would try to be. I suppose it was good training.

Nora's shoulders shined in the dashboard lights, and her dark eyes took on a life of their own when she looked at me. I tried not to stare. She noticed me looking but didn't flinch. For all I knew, she enjoyed it. "The ledger. It's in the study, correct?" I said. Basically, everything written down about Gibson's organization was in there. I remember watching Nora make notes and keep financial records on Gibson's clients in that ledger. She would either be in the study or the dining room, seated in front of that green banker's lamp, away from any distractions. It was staggering how Gibson was getting rich off his clients and their perverted fantasies, and all the while, Nora was keeping record. *Nobody knows the business like the bookkeeper, Calvin.* She had told me that back when I thought everything was cool. Scandalous, yes. But cool.

Once people figured out that Gibson was taking the evidence of what his clients had already paid for and extorting them for obscene amounts of money, that's when someone started the timer on him. In football, they would say that he was backed up into his own territory, it was fourth down and long with time running out, and all he had left was a *Hail Mary.*

I didn't want to stick around for that.

I waited at the last stop sign on Twenty-Third Street before the turn onto Wyoming. "How big is this thing, Nora?"

"Depends."

"On what?"

She brushed her hair back and looked ahead. "On how much you're willing to risk…and how much you want to spend."

I gripped the steering wheel. "Why can't you just tell me everything?"

"I don't trust you, Calvin."

"The feeling's mutual."

Headlights approached from behind. I took the turn onto Wyoming with heightened awareness. My eyes continued to adjust to the darkness, and I could see the house about a half block away. All the lights were off.

"Surprised there's not a lamb chop in the window," she said.

"Someone heard the same lecture I did."

"More than once."

I looked at her as I downshifted the BMW, driving by at a steady creep, looking for any movement, maybe a car in the drive behind the house or a sign that someone might be there. Minutes later, we pulled into the roundabout of Mitchell Park. Under the sound of crackling gravel, I killed the lights.

Nora took a deep breath and looked out her window. "I have the willies."

"I wonder if that's what all burglars say before a break-in?" It dawned on me that the car may look suspicious sitting by itself in Mitchell Park, warm and unattended. I decided I was paranoid and didn't give it another thought.

In my youth, I had a habit of sneaking out of the house to make out with a girl from the neighborhood or to smoke cigarettes or vandalize something; I hardly slept. To sneak back into the house undetected by my older sister, well, it took a certain amount of skill. Those easy skills, like removing window screens, and picking cheap locks could prove useful. However, this was not a restored barn like I grew up in, and I sure wasn't back on the block anymore. With that in mind, I had showed up a little better prepared. I brought a paint scraper, a pair of pliers, a Swiss Army knife, and that day's newspaper to wrap up anything important, since the weather reports called for rain.

We made it to Wyoming Avenue and Nora turned and looked behind us. I listened intently and tried to get in tune with the surroundings. My hands took on a mild tremor, and my mouth dried up like I was in a dentist's chair. We were ready. Even considering the suspicious look on Nora's face, we were really going to do this.

The driveway led back behind the home and was covered by low-hanging branches of large oaks. We made our way toward it and then stopped just past a row of hedges. I held my hand up for Nora to stop.

"Let's go," she said.

I could see the driveway, the street, and the house.

I took one last look at her and thought *setup*. I knew what was in it for Mr. Gibson, but what would be in it for her?

No matter what, when it came to Nora, I couldn't be too cautious.

***

Nora had assured me the ledger, as well as a box of credit card receipts, was in a built-in bookshelf behind the desk in the study. I simply had to break in through the garage and walk through the kitchen, down a hallway, past the living room and guest bath, and finally to a set of French doors that led to the study.

I took three tries with the paint scraper and the lock wouldn't open. Nora's eyes showed alarm, as she nervously looked around.

"Easier if you had a set of keys," I said.

"I never got them back from Philip."

On the fourth try, the lock popped open.

"About time." She scanned the backyard and patio area, while I knelt with a flashlight and considered the garage floor. "I want to come."

"We can't change the rules now," I said. "You notice anything, hide."

"Where?"

"You'll figure it out."

I walked inside the garage and let my eyes adjust. It was a two-car garage with window inserts on either side of the door that let in enough street light to keep me from tripping. It smelled a bit like fuel and dirt; knowing Gibson, he probably had his own landscaper. I thought maybe there would be at least one car in the garage, but it was empty. That meant he was paying for four spaces in the Foxhall basement garage, and that had to be awfully expensive. There was steel racking along the inside wall, stacked with catering equipment: serving trays, champagne buckets, boxes of glassware, flatware, food warmers, and steam tables, all remnants of his legendary parties.

The kitchen door was two steps up from the garage, leading to the main floor. I tried the handle., and it was unlocked. "Thank you."

Nora peeked in the garage. "I hate it out here." Without warning, a set of headlights shined in our direction. They were on Wyoming Avenue and getting closer. I ran outside for Nora and pulled her close to me. The car crept toward the house, while we hid behind one of the oaks. It was a D.C. patrol car.

"Oh no," Nora said.

"Quiet," I whispered. "Just routine." We were hunched down behind a short wooden fence, like kids playing a prank. The fence separated the back of the driveway from a stone patio. We couldn't have been more than fifty feet from the cops as they drove by.

"Now what?" she asked.

"Maybe they were just out on patrol."

"But they were driving so slow."

"Yeah, but no flood lights." I waited until they were out of sight. "I think we're good."

"This time I'm coming," she said. After a lengthy stare, I knew I couldn't win that argument. We waited another minute until things became still and quiet again. I closed the back door and followed Nora into the garage, up the stairs, and into the house. With the stale scents of cigar smoke and must, the house could use some open windows and a good cleaning.

I handed her my flashlight as we walked through the kitchen. I placed my tools and the newspaper on the kitchen table and followed her to the study. Nora pulled one door open and we slid inside. The large antique desk that I remembered seeing was centered near the back wall. The green lamp and cigar ashtray, as well as an open leather briefcase, sat atop it.

"The ledger?" I said.

"No." She opened the filing cabinet that sat near the south window and held the small flashlight over the drawer.

"Cover the light," I said.

"Don't tell me what to do."

221

She continued to fumble through some file folders, and then I watched her open the middle drawer. I walked back to the built-in bookcase and tried to make out some other documents and folders. I came up empty. Nora made her way to the far wall, half of which was lined with more bookshelves. The other half was a brag wall of framed pictures of Gibson with then Vice President Bush, the Defense Secretary, and the Japanese Prime Minister. Instinctively, I followed her over and watched as she twisted the Bush photo frame like a dial until it came loose.

"Hold this," she said.

"Oh, of course. Only Gibson." I watched again as she spun the dial of a small safe that was imbedded behind the picture. I assumed that the house had already been searched. *How could the Feds miss the credit card evidence and how could they not realize he had a hidden safe? Maybe they were looking for something else? Something more incriminating.*

She opened the safe and pulled out a brown file pocket and checked its contents. My eyes were locked on the office window. We needed to hurry.

Nora replaced the framed photo and began looking for something on the built-in bookshelves.

"What now?" I said.

"I want to wipe my prints."

"Your prints are all over this house."

"Yeah, but this is Exhibit A," she said. "Here, use your shirt and do it. I have to use the restroom."

Upon hearing that, I held out my arm and stopped her. "You're going to use the restroom during a robbery?"

222

"It's not a robbery, Calvin. I practically lived here."

"Technically, it's a robbery, especially since the Feds have already been here. That, and you're holding Exhibit A, remember?"

"Be right back," she said and slipped under my arm.

As I shook my head, I found some tissue and wiped the frame of the photo of Gibson with the other dignitaries. While I looked at everyone in the photo, I could see a reflection from the streetlight outside. The reflection showed the front yard, the stone retaining wall along the sidewalk…and the silhouette of a large man approaching the house.

Philip.

Chapter Thirty-five

Using my foot, I propped the French door open. I could see Philip's reflection in the glass as he entered the house. He was out of my view for a moment as he walked down the hall. He entered the kitchen and stood over the table with his back to me. Any second, Nora would flush the toilet, and I would have to do something. We had come to the tipping point with Eli, and if Philip knew it, then everybody knew it. He wasn't what you would call *in the know* in Washington, but he had to be desperate to get what he could and cover his tracks. Since leaving the Secret Service, Philip had started running with some questionable people and got paid to "handle business," which eventually led him to Gibson. After that, he played the game as though it was every man for himself.

So, what was his interest at Kalorama? And was he packing heat?

Seeing him standing over the kitchen table, I remembered that's where I had left my tools. Philip shined a pocket flashlight at the table and took quite an interest. I felt sick to my stomach because I realized that the newspaper was from that very day. Philip was a brute, there's no denying that, but he wasn't stupid. He must have had some suspicion already that there was a break-in, but once he saw the date on the newspaper, he had to know he wasn't alone.

He was only a step away when three things occurred. The first was him saying softly, *Tuesday*, luckily it took him a second to process the significance. The second thing was Nora making her presence known with the rippling, swirling sound of the toilet, and the third was me slinging the desk lamp's gold cord around his neck.

I didn't believe in ambushes or surprise attacks, no more than I did a sucker punch, but this guy was willing to kill me and who knows what he would do with Nora, or what he had already done.

The only thing tighter than that cord was copper wire.

Advantage Ducane.

I pulled the cord as hard as I could, but Philip drove us backwards into the wall and caught me with an elbow that sent me to the floor. The wind had been knocked out of me, and I panicked. He was now on top of me, slamming his fist into my jaw. "Should have killed you when I had the chance, kid." He had me. Nora had orchestrated a trap. They brought me here to die. As I fought to breathe, I reached in desperation for something, anything. His grip tightened on my throat, and blood had run into my eyes. I could only see Philip and his cold, swollen face as he applied more pressure. All the mistakes and lies of my double life had formed one large regret. And Nora was behind it. I started to fade. I could barely make out Philip reaching back for another punch. An object appeared above him, something sparkling and vivid. I thought it might be a hallucination until it smashed on Philip's swelled head with the sharp sound of exploding glass. He fell forward into a heap. Nora stood over us both. "Grab your things."

I stood up and stumbled over Philip, who lay motionless. I snatched the tools from the kitchen table, still fighting for air. I followed her out the kitchen door and through the garage. We weren't even near the edge of the property when the first two shots rang out.

Nora climbed over the ivy-covered wooden fence like an infantry soldier. Another shot cracked, this one closer. We had one more street to cross before reaching Rock Creek Park. We came out from behind one of the elaborate homes in Kalorama, and I saw the street signs for Tracy Place and Belmont Road.

"The park is farther than I thought," she said. We were behind a government building that had wrought-iron fencing around its driveway. Several embassies were in Kalorama, but you never got used to seeing them. Even when you're outrunning gunfire. A collection of trees beyond the fence gave us some cover. "The car would be nice," she said.

"If only." I peeked to see if Philip was still in pursuit.

"We've got to move," Nora said, "but they'll look for us in the park."

"Aren't we just trying to stay alive right now? What embassy is this?"

"Does it matter?" She looked past me and down the street again.

I tugged on her shirt to turn her toward me. I needed to look in her eyes. "Thank you, Nora."

226

She looked at the ground with a coy reluctance. "You would've done the same."

We were a block away from the Gibson residence, and the streets were silent. Whether Philip was looking for us or not, I knew one thing: we had to move.

***

We made it to the park before being detected. I kept a tight hold on the ledger.

Nora had earned my trust again after saving me from Philip. I don't think she knew how close I had come. For a moment, I was certain the two of them were conspiring, and that I might have ended up dead or missing like other people in Gibson's world. If Philip had his way, I would have.

We stood on a hill that overlooked the quiet, winding parkway. "I doubt we can flag down a cab," I said. "Or should we hike our way back to a Metro station and blend in?"

"Blend in at three a.m.?"

My mom was under the impression that I was spending the night at a friend's, so I was hopeful that she wasn't home worrying. Lately, it was one lie after another, and I had little doubt that it would all catch up to me. My current situation being a prime example.

"This spot looks familiar," Nora said. The road descended around the area where we were standing and then sloped off into the darkness.

I leaned on a large rock that she used to help herself down to a path in the woods. "I didn't like leaving the car in Mitchell Park, but I couldn't make up my mind."

"It's probably in an impound lot by now," she said.

"That's a safe bet." I played the night's events over in my head. *The night I nearly became a murderer.*

We looked down on the parkway in both directions, and not a single car had passed. I knocked mud from my shoes and met her eye to eye.

"You okay?" I said.

"I'm okay."

Reaching my hand into my back pocket, I felt something: a keychain. The keys to the Supra.

Chapter Thirty-six

"Do you think Eli will come clean?" I said.

"Knowing him? I doubt it."

We were close enough to the parkway that we could see the occasional road sign. It was getting near daybreak, and commuters were starting to appear. The illumination from a vehicle's headlights was welcome, as it let us see the trail ahead. An incline in the path led us to a small sign near a split in the trail.

Nora read aloud: "Soapstone."

"Say again?"

"If we take this trail up the hill, we'll be on Albemarle."

"I know Albemarle."

"We'll have to walk a few blocks to Tenleytown."

"Do we have a choice?"

"This is as close as we're going to get," she said. "Otherwise, we'll have to backtrack." She looked at me. "Hate for both of us to be paranoid, but what if we get questioned?"

"Let's not go looking into the crystal ball now, Nora. Besides, what are the chances?"

She got up close and looked into my eyes. "With our luck? Pretty good."

"Where's the strong-willed girl from Virginia that I've come to know? The slim chance that we get questioned, arrested, whatever, we deny everything. Wait, did someone forget how to lie?"

Nora's angry dark eyes cut me in two.

We walked back to the Tenleytown Metro, looking down every street with vigilance. The Supra was right where I'd left it. Some early risers were starting their daily routines. The sight of a cop caused Nora to tense up. "Hold my hand," I said. Nora obliged, and like that, we appeared to be a couple out on an early morning walk.

As we approached the car inside the garage, I said, "I wonder if a cop ran the plates?"

"It's Eli's car. A little too early to be seizing his assets."

"Here's hoping."

She stood in front of me, flat-footed, carrying her sandals, her hair tangled.

"You're a mess."

She looked me over. "You're no Prince Charming."

I threw the ledger on the backseat and got inside. As we pulled out of the garage, I said, "Can I say something?"

"Do you need permission?"

"I need you to hear me out."

"Well, let's have it then."

"Nora, you've been leading the way so to speak, and you've helped me. Been there when I really needed you."

"Okay."

"Well, we can't go any further into this mess. All this unraveling is because of Eli, and he knows it. That's why he's the one that's hiding out. But that's all about to change." I looked at her. "I can't do it without you. And you can't do it without me."

"Calvin, I'm grateful that you've hung in there, even after I told you to leave. If I were alone in this thing, with Eli in denial and Philip trying to muscle his way out, who knows where I'd be. Setting you up was the furthest thing from my mind, but there would've been a lot of heat on me if I didn't. It's a cheap, selfish excuse, but it's honest."

"I get it." At the stoplight near the Sidwell Friends School, I searched for something to say. "I thought one day I'd ask you to tell me about your experiences, but honestly, that's not how I want to remember you."

"I'm sorry, Calvin."

"No need to be sorry."

When it came to Eli, I was confident that Nora could work with him, and I felt that the short conversation we just had might have secured an agreement that we were now partners. The problem was, I didn't know what he had in mind for the two of us. Let alone for himself.

Chapter Thirty-seven

On the run. That was life now. From an optimistic view, all the running around might make me a good parent someday. *It might.*

I turned the shower on in my grandma's guest bathroom and looked forward to cleansing myself of all the filth covering my body and soul. I dropped my clothes and squeezed toothpaste onto my dry toothbrush. Nora had parked behind Foxhall and told me to meet her at Gibson's as soon as possible. Dressed and ready in a flash, I took the service elevator up to the third floor. While I made the long walk down the hall, I harkened back to the night that Nora had set me up. It had to be easy for them to accomplish: take an impressionable fool and dangle a carrot in front of him. Promise him a life of intrigue and wealth, and he won't say no. Now, it's just an envelope away. How much would you pay for something valuable that belonged to you, if you didn't want anyone to see it?

Mr. Gibson's condo door was cracked open, as though he were home. The sound of Nora's voice echoed down the hall, and she was in distress yet again. A hollowness entered my stomach. I ran down the hall and, as I got closer, I heard a man's voice yelling at her. I burst through the open door and found myself standing just steps from Oliver, the kid from the photo who looked like me.

Mr. Gibson's supposed *son*. Callboy is more like it.

"Can I help you?" he said, glaring at me. Nora stood across the room, near the office doorway. Her pained expression made my blood boil. Her arms were draped across her body, and she avoided eye contact with him.

"I'll bet you can," I said.

He took a step toward me. "What the fuck is that supposed to mean?"

"Stop it, Oliver," Nora said.

He chewed on a toothpick, and a thick vein split his forehead in half. His blonde hair was slicked back, showing off his glossed-over eyes. My guess was he was another druggy.

I looked for a pistol, thinking maybe he was packing and had been sent by Philip. I thought of how to confuse him. He must not have been clued in on anything by Mr. Gibson, so he had to be looking for us. Nora knew Mr. Gibson was still out of the country. This meant Philip and anyone else involved in his ring were expendable. That included Oliver. "I'll bet you have a lot of unanswered questions. But Eli isn't around. We heard he left the country."

"Fuck off." Oliver was built a lot like me but thin, and maybe an inch taller. He had those Midwestern looks. I wondered for a moment that, in his short life, how he would have found Gibson, or vice versa. For that matter, how anyone, including Nora, had ever found Gibson. It was too late to empathize.

"What's your name?" Oliver said.

"You'll remember here shortly…if you decide to stay. It's your choice."

Oliver bit down on the toothpick and looked at Nora and then back at me, waiting for someone to show their cards.

"We didn't meet here to walk the dog, Oliver," I said.

He took another look at Nora. "Why are you here?"

"I'm surprised you don't already know," she said. "This place is about to get raided. Sooner rather than later. They're investigating Eli. He left the country. You may want to do the same."

He stared at the ground as if trying to solve a puzzle. Then he looked at me with contempt. "Ever since you came into the picture."

"Your choice."

"I don't believe you."

"Then stay. You're an innocent man, right?" I walked past him and into the office. I looked at the picture above the bar again. *Was that really him?* Nora didn't move. I continued to stare at the picture of who I thought was Oliver in his youth. I listened as Nora spoke to him. "A friend at the Times gave me a lead that both his homes were going to get raided. I'm here to grab some of his belongings, which is risky at this point. When Eli will be back in town is anyone's guess."

"That's nice, Nora," Oliver said as he lit a cigarette. "If Eli comes back, and the three of you settle the score between yourselves, congratulations. But if I find him first, you can be rest assured you'll never see him again."

"Oliver, wait—"

"Those are my terms."

Oliver put his cigarette out on Eli's rug and walked out the door.

"That was rather tense," I said.

Nora was in the foyer trying to clean the burn mark on the rug. "Oliver has an old vendetta against Eli."

"He sure made that clear."

Nora walked over to the desk and sat down, motioning for me to join her. She tugged on one of the bottom drawers of Mr. Gibson's desk and found it locked. She fumbled through a few more, and after opening the top drawer, said, "Oh boy."

I looked over her shoulder and saw the paraphernalia from Mr. Gibson's coke habit: a rolled up hundred-dollar bill, a small, oval bathroom mirror, empty baggies, and razor blades.

"You're surprised?" I said.

"He didn't do it in front of me that often."

"He did it in front of me. Plenty."

"The man sure liked his…."

"Hookers and blow?"

"More like callboys." She tapped her fingernails along the desk, looking around. With a squint of her eye, she racked her brain. Standing up, she nudged me aside and walked back to the wet bar. She got up on the tips of her toes but couldn't reach the top shelf.

"Come over here please," she said. "Check for a set of keys up there."

I reached up and fished around until I found them.

Using the keys, she opened a large bottom drawer of the desk, revealing over a dozen VHS tapes. "The motherload."

Using a remote control, she turned on the television that was mounted in the corner. Under it was an attached VCR. She inserted one of the tapes. Knowing what I was about to witness, I clenched my fists. She pushed *Play*.

The digital display of the date appeared in the corner of the screen, indicating the recording was two years old. The picture quality made it hard to see, but there was a man in a suit in a large bedroom. He was taking his tie off when a young man in a white T-shirt walked past him. From the camera's point of view, it had to be set up behind a one-way mirror. The 'client' had no idea he was being filmed. For that matter, the callboy might not have either.

"Kalorama," she said.

"Turn it off."

"It's important that you see this."

I became wheezy and wanted to vomit. "Nora, please turn it off."

"Okay, okay," she said. "There are dozens of them." She ran her hand along the back of her neck and looked away from me. "And there's one of me. And now...there's one of us."

She came around the desk and leaned on it with her back to me. The room had warmed with sunlight. Nora

236

shook her head as if to ward off any regrets of the past, of any involvement with Gibson. "There's probably over seven figures collected in there. And you've only seen the credit card receipts. You should see the cash."

As a valet parker, living on two-dollar tips, I had a hard time even imagining. I watched her lock the front door and walk into the kitchen. I could hear the icemaker dispensing cubes. About a minute later, she left the bar and came back with two half-filled tumblers of orange juice and, based on my first sip, a healthy dose of vodka.

"Hopefully, last night will be the worst of it," she said.

"If we stick around much longer, that could change."

"Calvin, I spent two summers interning on the Hill with two different firms, one of them being Ingersoll. I was just a kid. Once I graduated, they offered me entry-level as a marketing assistant, which I accepted. I wanted to live in the city, and I wanted to continue in public relations, but I could barely make it on the salary. I didn't want to get involved in blackmail or prostitution or racketeering or any of this nonsense. I met Eli at a black-tie fundraiser. He had an entourage. He was with these Japanese businessmen and a media star and the former CIA Director. He was friends with my boss and seemed like everyone knew him." She sipped her drink. "He had exceptional taste and was so charming. It was like I was bewitched. He invited me back to the house after the fundraiser. My boss said I didn't have a choice. Since then, nothing's been the same. We got there, and he had waiters in white gloves and tuxedos. He had lobster and champagne. Lamb chops and cocaine. Lamb chops, Calvin. Just like Perle Mesta."

"I thought he didn't do coke in front of you."

"It didn't stop his guests. They loved the speedballs."

"Gotcha."

Nora twirled the straw in her drink and took another sip. "It was around midnight that about five of us got into a limo. He said we were going to tour the White House. Everyone felt great, laughing, politely drunk, but no one, not even the four-star general, thought he was serious. And then we walked right in the goddamned White House. I can't describe the feeling that I had that first time. You remember. How did that make you feel? How were we supposed to not trust a man who took us to the White House at midnight, Calvin? Tell me."

"I was all in after that trip."

"So, he sends flowers and a gift certificate to some swanky spa downtown. It includes a note to come to the house the following week for a dinner party, tells me he wants me to meet some of his friends. He sends Philip to my house in the BMW, the one I'm driving now. I was—"

"Nora, you know I have a similar story. The question is, what are you now?"

"I think you know what I am, Calvin." She took a long sip from her drink and looked around the condominium. "I'm the token woman. And that's got me worried more than anything."

238

Chapter Thirty-eight

The way everything had transpired in the last forty-eight hours, it was only fitting I would run into Mr. Gibson. Whether overseas or wherever, he would come back, at the very least for his money. My hunch was that he would reach out to Nora or appear at Foxhall or the club—even if it meant that he would be risking arrest. That said, it was anyone's guess if the authorities had enough grounds to detain him for questioning.

I told a few more lies to my family with the hopes I would buy some time and dig myself out of the hole I had dug. Nora and I were on the same page, but Oliver was a wild card. We were heading into Independence Day, and the city was heating up.

As Nora had mentioned earlier, many of Gibson's clients had questions, mostly about money. Plain and simple, he owed them; he owed them a lot. And there were people who owed him because of extortion and blackmail. But that wasn't exactly public knowledge. If Eli Gibson had any dirt on you—I'm talking *dirt*—he had you by the balls. Who was going to try to muscle a guy who had videotapes of them having sex with a prostitute? He was the most dangerous man in town, at least to the people whose names were in his ledger, written in ink. We were engaged in a sizable web of corruption that involved a list of powerful people. None of it was going away, and something had to give.

While the waiting game for Eli continued, the people on that list all had one thing in common: they were nervous.

***

"Eli's back in town," Nora said. She was standing in her kitchen, wearing red running shorts and a black sports bra. We were on better speaking terms since our conversation after leaving Tenleytown, but you could sense a lingering resentment between us. I thought that maybe we were both agitated over all the uncertainty. I envisioned the moment she shattered the wine decanter over Philip's head, just as I was about to eat one of his fists. She was there when I needed her most, but then she wanted me to watch blackmail sex tapes. As far as I was concerned, our trust went back to hanging in the balance.

"He's staying at the Willard of all places, under an alias," she said. "He doesn't sound like himself, but he still wants to meet. Not sure how I feel about it."

I started pacing, "Has he seen the paper?"

"He mentioned it. He's not rattled at all. That's what happens when someone's in complete denial. And he only wants me to show up."

"What? How about neither of us are showing up then. We can't take the risk, and considering that we stole his ledger, we may end up in the Potomac in a boat made of concrete."

240

"I think you've been watching too much television."

"Is he alone or is one of his strongarms with him?"

"It's anyone's guess," she said. "So, suppose Philip tells him that we made off with the ledger. He could be trying to lure us himself, but for all we know, someone could be holding a gun to his head."

"Didn't he do that to one of his—"

"That ship has sailed, Calvin." She walked out of the kitchen. On her way upstairs she said, "The focus is still on covering our tracks. That's pretty much it." I could hear her footsteps on the carpet as she ran up the stairs.

She had cut me off before I could bring up the story about a callboy who was supposedly kidnapped and then disappeared. Eli and his cohorts were never pinned for the crime, there was no investigation or press, but Eli Gibson's downfall only gained momentum. I found out later that the callboy was a friend of Oliver's, and he wasn't the only one who had gone missing. The corruption, the scandal, the *conspiracy*, it was way larger and way older than anyone involved would care to admit.

As much as Eli Gibson adored and admired Perle Mesta, his real motivation came from his intricate knowledge of the witch hunt of homosexuals working in government during the 1950s, otherwise known as *The Lavender Scare*. McCarthyism brought with it paranoia about communists working inside the American government. Joe McCarthy was making a list. The Lavender Scare was the idea that gays could be easily coerced or even blackmailed into sharing government secrets, and nearly all of them working in the

State Department and other agencies lost their jobs.

Blackmail. If Eli could have blackmailed Joe McCarthy himself, he would have. But that was neither here nor there. He was out of options for his prostitution and blackmail rings, and Joe McCarthy was pushing up daisies. Soon, he would discover that he *won't miss his water til the well runs dry*, and it was about that time. He was desperate and had few people to rely on. Even Nora or I coming to his rescue would do him no good. But he would continue, someway, somehow.

I heard the shower turn on and thought of Nora getting in and letting the water run over her body. Luckily, I had gained a bit of self-control, so I saved that daydream for another time. We had to put an end to our involvement with Gibson.

Hurry up, buttercup.

Chapter Thirty-nine

"Can we not meet him in his room?" I said, "considering his...state of mind."

"I thought the same thing. Told him we'd meet at the bar downstairs."

We walked through the Willard's lobby where President Ulysses S. Grant coined the term "lobbyist" in 1869, because he was constantly bothered by self-promoters while he enjoyed a cigar and brandy. Grant and Lincoln, even Martin Luther King Jr., had stayed at the Willard. But when it came to Eli Gibson, he had fallen woefully short in becoming one of those with such power and political influence. We walked the hallway toward the famous Round Robin Bar and heard laughter and the dinging of glassware. He was seated at a table opposite the bar and had his back to the wall.

"Anyone follow you here?" he said, his voice croaked like a parched hitchhiker. Nora sat down across from him and we ordered drinks.

"Just us, Eli," she said. "Where have you been?"

"Why, somebody looking for me? Quite an ugly sound from that pretty face." He was dressed in dark clothes and hadn't shaved in some time. His skin was rough and had tightened as though he'd lost weight.

243

"Never mind all that, Mr. Gibson," I said. "If they find you here, and you know who 'they' means, you'll never see the light of day again." He shrugged his shoulders. "The Kalorama ledger, black and whites, and the credit card log are all in our possession. So, you're welcome."

They were both looking at the table while a server delivered drinks. Nobody said anything. Gibson surveyed the room, looking around like he'd just been released from solitary confinement. When I thought about all the paranoia that I'd experienced, I couldn't imagine what he had to be dealing with. Topping that off with being on copious amounts of drugs and alcohol, he was not in a good place.

"Believe me, Calvin," Nora said, "he doesn't scare easy. Isn't that right, Eli?" He slouched in his seat and smiled. I found myself grinding my teeth, sitting there having drinks with a guy who made his living by preying on other people, exploiting their weaknesses and documenting it all. That was the hook. Then, all they could do was pay up.

"We have too much work to do to be scared, right?" he said, scratching his stubble. "Our friends from State and their guests will be visiting soon and staying here. It should be a stellar night if we can get everything set up properly."

Nora spoke softly, "That's not happening, Eli. What's done is done. Now, it's a matter of what the investigation turns over and what your lawyers can do." I sat back and listened. *Was he planning on hiding out in a hotel until he knew the outcome? No doubt he was delusional.*

"Nora, darling," he said, "I'm having two suites booked for the occasion. I'll need you to go do a walk through and check everything out." He flashed a devilish grin and ran his hand along her arm. "I need you to do what you do best." He gazed at her to see if his charm had worked. Nora was strong, but who knows what kind of stranglehold he had on her.

"I don't want you ignoring what is happening around you, Eli." She leaned into him and spoke in a slow whisper, "They're closing in on you and they can likely do whatever they want in the process. They can bankrupt you, throw you in prison, or make you disappear, whatever they want. But if there's one thing you're short on, it's time."

Gibson sat up in his seat. "I've been working on this one all year. It's an enormous payday."

"Mr. Gibson, are you listening to her? You need an exit strategy, and fast. We didn't come here for any kind of deal. Our work is done. If you and your entourage want to go sting the fucking Prince of Wales, I don't really give a damn. It's time to move on or we'll all go down together. So, you want a deal? I've got one for you. I bring you the ledger, you do what you want with it. Might I suggest burning it? In exchange, you give me the tape I've been asking for."

"How old are you again, son?"

"Old enough to know when I've been conned," I said. "Make sure you have the tape when I visit your room." Gibson wore a pathetic grin on his face. He was sitting there, just waiting for the next valet, the next callboy, bodyguard, or token woman. He was waiting for them to come in and clean up his mess while he contemplated how and where he would get his rocks off next.

I stood up to leave the bar.

"I'll meet your deal," he said. Those beady little eyes were back. "Sit back down, son."

He put his drink down and leaned into the table. "We'll do the exchange, but the two of you need to help my contractor get the rooms ready."

Nora rolled her eyes so quick they looked like marbles.

"We don't want anything to do with that," I said.

"Tomorrow morning, five a.m., room twelve-oh-one, then we'll do the exchange after it's all ready. That's the new deal. FDR would be proud, son." He stood up and finished his drink. He pulled a crisp hundred-dollar bill from a money clip, laid it on the table, and walked out.

I felt like we were stumbling into another trap. Gibson was running out of time, he was running out of friends and he was running out of money. That's not good in a city like Washington, and somehow, I was still involved.

***

The car's engine purred like a napping lion, helping me calm down. As we drove back to Arlington, Nora's head leaned back on the seat, her eyes fixed on somewhere distant, perhaps somewhere safer. She had been living a life of *it's almost over* for some time now. That was my impression at least.

"Why the hell are we involved in this at all?" I said. "Why don't we just call those two jerks from your firm and tip them off? Why don't we—"

"Because we're out of options, Calvin. Eli has everyone who's looking for him in the palm of his hand. This is his last setup in Washington, without a doubt. Plus, he's already established himself overseas." She pulled down the visor in front of her and hunted through her purse. "You know what else? As fast as a camera flash, he can change the lives of some very powerful people, not to mention make himself rich in the process."

"Well, he's doing it on his own this time. You can do as you wish, but I'm sure as hell not assisting him. He gets the ledger, we get the tape, then we build a bonfire somewhere and destroy it."

"Let's hope it's that simple."

Chapter Forty

"Cal," Nora said.

"I got it."

"Cal." She tapped the back of my shoulder.

"I got it."

I looked up as the first Metro ticket fed out of the machine to see two men in suits coming down the escalator, both in dark sunglasses, both looking for someone. We were taking the train from Friendship Heights to her place since the preparation for the Fourth of July had the city in a gridlock.

"You know them?" I said.

"Hurry."

I pushed the flimsy ten-dollar bill into the machine, and it was rejected. I looked behind me and saw the men walking toward us; they were within a hundred feet.

"Hurry," she said.

I fed the machine again and it paused. "C'mon."

The machine finally spit out the ticket. We walked with a purpose to the gate and inserted our tickets. The two men were gaining on us, but not running. They could've very well had their eyes on someone else, but it didn't appear that way. They wanted us.

"Who the hell are they?" I said.

We rounded the corner to the platform, and the

sound of a policemen's radio entered my ear. There, twenty feet away from us, was a Metro cop on the beat. He walked toward the ticket gate. The rumble of the approaching train filled the room. Nora took my arm and pulled me to the end of the platform. The train ripped into the tunnel. Each car shook the ground and flashed light into our eyes. The announcer came over the loudspeaker, *"This is the Redline to Metro Center."* We stood on the opposite side of a large, stone pillar. Nora glanced back behind us as the train came to a slow stop.

"They're Secret Service," she said. "Former."

I glanced back and didn't see them. The train door opened. A rush of people exited. The voice on the overhead gave the final call, *"Redline to Metro Center."*

"I'll take your word for it," I said. "What do you want to do?"

"Meet in Rockville."

"What? I'm not leaving you."

"Catch the next train. We can't be together."

"Let me talk to them," I said.

"No, avoid them." She looked at the ground. "Hide in the crowd. Go to Tenleytown. Come back and meet in Rockville." I watched her enter the train just as the doors shut. She looked out at me with calm determination, and the train sped away.

***

I zigzagged through the crowd and was opposite the platform from the two men. A second train sounded its horn, and the flash from its headlights entered the tunnel. People stood up from the benches and moved to the left side of the platform. I pulled a newspaper hanging from a garbage can and sat down. The horn sounded again, and a train entered the tunnel, *"This is the Redline to Shady Grove"* came over the loudspeaker. It was then that I realized Nora was on the wrong train and would have to get off and come back toward Maryland. I began to wonder how long it would be until she figured it out herself. With my head down, I kept my nose in the paper. On the first page turn, I noticed two sets of dark shoes facing me on the platform.

"Mr. Ducane," the deep, baritone voice said.

I looked the man in the eye. "Can I help you?"

"Mr. Ducane, are you connected to Eli Gibson?"

"I'm afraid you have the wrong person. Now, if you'll excuse me...."

The larger of the two men pulled out a badge. "We'd like to ask you a few questions." A middle-aged couple who were sitting close to me stood up and walked away.

"My name isn't Ducane." The train let out a screech and pulled away.

"You sure do resemble someone we're looking for," the shorter of the two said, looking me over.

"It happens." I walked away. The stairwell was right in front of me, and I didn't see them when I turned around.

Keeping my eye out, I slipped into a men's room stall. I couldn't get the look of the tall man out of my head. He was about six-foot-three and had a square jaw. His eyes seemed to almost tremor with anger. They were an eccentric dark blue color and were sunken into his skull. I wanted to punch something, to punch out all my anger and hostility. This wasn't fun anymore; I had had enough.

I opened one of the stall doors and could hear a policeman's radio behind me. In walked the two men, with the Metro cop right behind them. *I should've known. I should've known.* The cop watched them enter and shook his head as he closed the door behind him. They must've paid him to watch the door.

I walked toward the back of the room, and the tall one with the eyes came after me. "There's no door over there," he said. His partner approached on my left.

I pushed on the second stall door, but it was jammed shut. The tall one continued walking toward me. His accomplice stood within arm's reach. The thick lines in his face intensified.

"How do I say this politely?" he said. "You're coming with us, so don't make this difficult."

The tall one eyed me closely. "Guess what, kid? I know you're with Gibson. Now, you're going to take us to the ledger, or they'll find you in the deep woods of Virginia sometime next week, you got it?"

"Fuck you, you cock-eyed asshole!"

He punched me in the face, just missing my left eye.

I had my back to the wall, and the last stall door

opened. A skinny black man in a loose Army jacket and a worn Redskins hat stumbled out, his shoes sliding over the gray, tile floor. He put his arms up and tried to squeeze between myself and the two goons.

"Don't mind me, fellas," he said. "Just passing through. This is none of my—"

I shoved the man into the two goons and punched the tall one square on the chin. The risky play allowed me to make a mad dash for freedom.

I slammed through the men's room door and barreled past the surprised Metro cop standing watch. I decided that the escalator would slow me down, so I ran for the stairs. The hours and hours of sprinting up Congressional's stairs had paid off.

The cop ran after me, but he didn't stand a chance. I noticed him turn back at the base of the stairs. He pulled his radio and ran toward the restrooms. It was enough time for me to make it up three flights and out on the street. Pigeons scattered, and people ran from me, clearly not used to a normal commuter in a full sprint. I crossed over Wisconsin Avenue, ran down a side street, and managed to flag down a cab.

"Tenleytown," I said, as I fell into the backseat, still laboring for breath.

The cabbie leaned over and looked at me. "You could walk dare, yah know."

"Yeah, I know," I said. "What time you got?" I scanned his dashboard and couldn't find the time anywhere. He pulled through a back alley and checked his watch.

252

"Ten minutes to three. You okay?"

"Yeah, I'm all right. Why, do I look stressed?"

Chapter Forty-one

The train from Tenleytown to Rockville swayed back and forth, and I thought about water and maybe even a cigarette. There was no sense in replaying the events that just took place. Everywhere I went now, I'd be mistaken for someone, accused of something or thought of as a conspirator in something. I wasn't having spells of paranoia anymore—I was living in constant paranoia. Big difference.

Nora was waiting on the platform when I arrived. She faced the opposite direction, but her silhouette and flowing dark hair made her easy to spot. The train slowly crept back to the platform when she noticed me.

"How long until you figured you were headed the wrong way?" I said. The hiss of the Metro train hydraulics and voices of other passengers echoed around us.

"I'm just glad you made it."

"Almost didn't."

Nora looked closely at me and her smile disappeared. "Look at me. What happened to your eye?" She touched underneath my eye with her thumb, and I flinched.

"They tried to beat me up in the men's room. They asked me how I'm connected to Eli. And they know about the files, the tapes, everything."

"You're lucky they didn't kill you." She moved close to me and looked down the platform.

"Those are the moonlighters, aren't they? Confusing because one of them flashed a badge."

"I remember the tall one escorting us on a tour of the White House. He'd be at Kalorama also, but never socializing. Quite the creep, he is. Are you sure you're okay?"

For a second, it felt like Nora was genuinely concerned for my wellbeing. It gave me something to cling to. *Hope*, I guess.

"I'm all right."

***

Darkness owned the streets the following morning when we descended upon the Willard Hotel. I spent the night on Nora's couch, so I wore the same clothes. She was wearing a loose-fitting lavender V-neck shirt over white denim shorts that she folded at the bottoms. "You've got a style for every occasion, don't you?"

"Focus," she said.

We pulled in the Willard's garage, and parked near the elevators.

We took the elevator to the twelfth floor, where we walked down the long, elegant hallway. "You're late," a man told Nora as we met at the hotel room door. Mark was his name, and he wasn't much for handshakes. He had been waiting for us in one of the two penthouse suites that would be set up for video and audio surveillance. He had a dirty white beard and wore jeans, a faded red polo, and beat-up work boots.

255

In the parlor room, he had what appeared to be utility trunks, two of them. The kind you'd see roadies loading onto buses on a concert tour. Although I could sense how annoyed Nora was even being there, I was looking forward to seeing how one of Gibson's operations was set up. Just the idea of it all gave me the creeps, but I was fascinated.

Mark peered down the hall, closed the door, and then locked the deadbolt. "Let's get to work."

He put on his toolbelt and changed a bit in his cordless drill. He threw two orange extension cords out and walked off the distance across the parlor, marked the cords with black electrical tape, and then wrapped them up. Plastic zip ties went in his hip pocket along with electrical tape of three different colors.

"Are you watching this?" I said.

"I hope you are," Nora said. "You're the apprentice."

"I'm sure I could figure it out."

"He uses all the best equipment," Nora said. "The kind of stuff they use for banks and divorce proceedings."

"Divorce?"

"People trying to catch each other cheating. They can use it as long as it's admissible in court." Looking down the hall, she lowered her voice. "Apparently he's a retired private detective and would be a lot richer if he'd gone out on his own, but Eli had other plans for him."

"Don't tell me…."

"Oh yeah," she said. "Set him up with some callboy from Spanish Harlem and taped the whole thing. He's been on the hook ever since. His number one skill though is still one of the hardest to find."

"What's that?"

"He knows how to keep his mouth shut."

That was something I hadn't really wrapped my head around with Eli and his group—*the secrets*.

Mark walked back into the foyer. He opened the second of the two trunks and pointed to a long toolbox. "Grab this and follow me." There was a hallway separating two bedrooms. I reached for the toolbox, and its weight was equivalent to a full keg of beer.

I gave it the best I had and followed him into the far bedroom. I placed the toolbox on the floor and took a step back.

"Hand me a ratchet with a three-quarter-inch drive," he said.

"Should I just guess?"

Mark wiped sweat from his forehead. "You work for Gibson?" He got in front of me and fished for a wrench and adapter.

"In a roundabout way."

"I can tell," he said. "We've got to move the trunk and desk out of the way until I'm done in here, so give me a hand." We moved the trunk from the foot of the bed into the hallway between the bedrooms, and then we picked up the cherry wood desk and moved it enough to get to a large, framed piece of art: a painting of Calvin Coolidge, which was mounted on the wall and facing the bed. I held the painting in place while he used a measuring tape to make several marks with a pencil. After removing the artwork, he used a small mechanical saw to cut a square inside the original dimensions. We did similar work in the other bedroom. He then used mounting brackets and electrical tape to hold each video camera in place. From an adjoining closet, we ran extension cords to either bedroom and connected the two cameras.

In place of the art were one-way mirrors that complemented the penthouse suite. We had packed up the tools to do the exact same thing on the other wing of the hotel when there was a knock at the door.

***

Another knock. My only thought was Gibson.

Mark looked through the peephole and immediately looked back at Nora. "You got your charm socks on?"

Nora closed her eyes and sighed. She approached the door and looked to see who it was. She motioned for us to move away from the foyer. "If I'm not back in five, come get me." She tossed her hair, adjusted her breasts in her shirt, and slipped out the door. Being jealous about a girl who just recently was trying to ruin your life is a unique feeling all its own. And a stupid one at that.

"Whoever it is, they can't come in here," Mark said. "No one is allowed until after hours tonight, so...."

"I think I get it." I felt a cold stare as Nora's five minutes counted down in my head. Mark peered through the peephole. I began pacing. "What are they doing?"

The door opened, and Nora slid inside. She looked back and winked at the person in the hallway and closed the door. "I need money."

"What kind of money?" I said.

"Do you have anything on you?"

"Will a grand do?"

"It'll have to."

I fumbled into my wallet and counted out ten one-hundred-dollar bills and handed them to her. Something about the whole deal made her nervous. She slipped out the door.

"She's working her magic on the guy," Mark said. I looked out the peephole. Nora had the manager against the wall. She was flattering him into whatever she needed.

That's not her magic. Not even close

Chapter Forty-two

After completing a nearly identical job on the opposite penthouse, Nora and I left Mark and took the BMW out of the city. My apprenticeship in high-stakes blackmail was all but complete. What remained would be difficult, and it would involve sex trafficking. That hour was now upon us, and I had grown unwilling to play any part in it. For some time after, I would ask myself why I needed to know so badly. This was no cheap thrill. Thoughts of my family crept into my mind, causing me to be uptight, with nervous hands and a clenched jaw. But I could worry about my involvement once this was all over.

Nora drove me back to Foxhall. It was just past noon. She slowed down at the guard shack, so I could be identified by Carl. When I rolled down the window, he jumped out of his chair and walked outside, smiling as usual.

"Where you been, mon?" Carl said. He was a Jamaican guy, skin the color of coffee. He wore gold jewelry with his starched white *Foxhall* security shirt. He looked over at Nora and gave her a friendly smile.

"Carl, this is Nora."

"Yeah, I know. How you, Miss Nora?"

"I'm just fine, Mister Carl. You weren't sleeping in there, were you now?"

"Ha, you know I don't sleep at Foxhall, Miss Nora." I had a ten-dollar bill cupped in my right hand and looked behind us.

Reaching out to shake hands, I said, "Have you seen our old friend Mr. Gibson by chance?"

Carl took my hand and wrapped one arm over the car. He let out a long breath and leaned in, "You know that mon's in some trouble. People come here looking."

"People?" Nora said. "With badges?"

Carl looked back down the drive. "Something like that, yeah."

"Today?" I said.

"No, yesterday. Tree of dem."

"Anyone else?" Nora asked. "No Gibson?"

"Not yet. I tell him to call you, Miss Nora."

"Thanks, Carl. Have a good day."

"Take care now," he said.

Nora sped up the hill and around the roundabout. "They know he's in town."

"They?"

"The staff. Which means there are others. He's always been so careful, I don't know why he's running such a risk. I guess he wants to turn his nose up at everyone. Question for us is, what do we do now?"

"We go visit Uncle Jack," I said. "And hand everything over. We take off next week for Rehoboth. We're both safe. We didn't know what we were getting into, so—"

"So, we just trust this all to your Uncle Jack?" She wasn't buying it, and quite honestly, after giving it some thought, I wasn't either. "I'll tell you one thing, it's not going to go the way we're hoping."

"That, I can agree with." I looked across at her. "And what about tonight? Do we have a choice?"

"Our choice is simple. Either pull this off and not get caught, or look forward to cameras, microphones, and courtrooms…maybe worse." She looked at me with a firm resolve. "I'm picking you up at five, so be ready."

I got out of the car and watched her drive around the Foxhall roundabout. *If there were a time and opportunity to bail, that time would be now.*

***

"Hello, Fran." My words carried a faint echo inside the Foxhall entrance.

Fran stopped what she was doing and took her black-rimmed readers off. "Well, if it's not the elusive Mr. Ducane."

"Elusive?"

"Mr. Ducane. Calvin. Earlier today, we had some very important people here looking for one of our residents—a resident that I think you know quite well, actually." Somewhere, buried deep within her being, I was convinced there was a strict English teacher ready to crack my knuckles with a ruler. I was concerned she may have told

262

my family about my continued involvement with Mr. Gibson.

"And?"

"Calvin, these were men with guns. It may be hard for you to grasp," her voice lowered just short of a whisper, "but there is possible criminal activity happening here at Foxhall, and these men are determined to prosecute those involved."

"Jesus."

"Jesus can't help these people, Calvin. The reason I'm sharing this with you is because a while back, your mother was concerned about your, how should we say, your *socializing* here at the Foxhall. I'd hate for you to get caught up in something that you've been unaware of. Lucky for you, this person is out of town."

"I agree wholeheartedly."

Fran put her glasses back on. "Now, let me ask you, was this helpful?"

"Yes, ma'am," I said with a slight crack in my voice.

"Good. You're a smart young man, Calvin. You need to make good choices for yourself."

"I will, Fran. Thank you."

Fran had a look of pride in her eyes, like a poker player with a straight flush.

***

I opened the door of my grandma's condo like a burglar. I was expecting to see everyone, but I was alone. I was halfway up the stairs to shower when I heard a knock at the door. I stood on the staircase with a strange feeling. I thought of not answering, but it's not like the day could get any more unusual. Whoever it was kept knocking. I crept down the stairs and across the rug to the door. As I looked in the peephole, the person standing outside noticed and waved.

Gibson.

I never even thought whether I should open the door, it just happened.

"How the hell are you, handsome?" he said and walked inside. His dog Winston scampered in and made his way into the living room. Gibson must have got some rest. He may have even laid off the blow because he was more coherent than at our previous meeting, if only by a little. I kept my composure and looked out down the hall toward the lobby.

"Did Fran see you?"

"Who?"

"Never mind," I said. "I thought you were staying at the Willard."

"I'll get there soon enough."

He reeked of booze and showed signs of doing blow, as his eyes were painted white; my initial hunch was wrong. We stood on the rug in the foyer. He was in a black sport coat, much like the one Nora had picked out for me. He wore blue jeans and Brogues and still hadn't shaved. Inside the chest pocket of the jacket was an overstuffed white envelope.

264

"You can't. . .my mom and grandma—"

"Never mind grandmama, son. Two quick questions. Are the other rooms ready at the Willard, and who spoke to the Washington Times?"

"I'm not sure I follow."

Gibson yanked a pistol from his pocket and held it under my chin. It was the snub nose .38 Special that I'd seen in his desk. The sound of the hammer cocking told me he meant business.

"Don't you fuck with me," he said.

My body shook. I couldn't control it. I thought of my family. I thought of my mom. I had taken this adventure too far, and now it was going to cost me everything. *Get the gun. Get the fucking gun.*

I looked him square in his eyes. "Who else are you planning to kill, Eli?" I took a deep breath and tried to swallow. "And tonight. It can't happen without you. Do yourself a favor, put the gun away and get back to the Willard. Your tracks have been covered, just like we told you. All that's left is tonight. You leave there, you board a plane. . .and go live your life."

He didn't respond.

Only some of what I said was true, but I was negotiating for my life. A few seconds passed, and he looked up the stairs and then back at me. He slowly pulled the gun away and slid it back into his jacket. I stood firm and didn't move. He walked by me and whistled for Winston. I heard voices in the hallway and panicked. I could only imagine:

Mom, you remember Mr. Gibson, right? He's the guy with the prostitution ring who blackmails people and sneaks folks in the White House and does coke with hookers and dirty politicians? Anyway, I thought he could stay for dinner, if that's okay.

After the dog appeared from beyond the couch, Gibson walked over to my grandma's baby grand piano and sat down. "Well, what do we have here." He began playing classical music. He played as though he were performing at Carnegie Hall. I thought he might break out a clarinet. Intense, sophisticated music filled the room. Winston had jumped up on one of the blue chairs and was lying beside a throw pillow with his ears perked up.

"You've got to go," I said. "I'll see you and Nora later, but you. . .you have to leave."

He stopped playing the piano and looked at me with a disappointed stare. He sniffed a bump of coke out of a brass keychain and stood up.

"Not bad, eh?" he said through a wise grin.

I walked ahead of him toward the door. "You missed your calling."

"How's the senator doing?"

"Does it really matter? Look, my family will be home soon. They'll lose it if they see you. You've got to go." One minute he has me at gunpoint, the next he's playing Mozart on the piano and entertaining his little white dog.

He pulled the envelope from his pocket. It was loaded with hundred-dollar bills. "Have I not rewarded you, son?"

"Not necessary, Mr. Gibson. Save it. You're going to need it."

He dropped Winston and began pulling the jacket off. He took the gun out and stuffed it partially into his jeans, causing me another dreadful rush of panic.

He handed me the jacket. "Here, see if it fits. Something to remember me by."

"You really need to go," I slipped the jacket on and stood there staring at him. He fumbled with the envelope and finally looked at me. "Besides, I'll be there tonight."

"What do you mean you'll be there?" he said.

"Did you forget?"

He tilted his head like a dog watching an ice cream cone.

"You have something of mine," I said. "And I'm coming to get it."

"Oh, right, right," he said without a worry. "And you have something of mine."

"I plan on holding up my end of the bargain. And there is only one ledger. I can guarantee that. Can you guarantee there's only one tape? No copies?"

"Only one," he said. He did not look away, but I still had a hard time believing him. "Looks good. Stretch your arms out." I really didn't care about the jacket. *Please, just go.*

I did as he asked, keeping the gun and his hands in sight.

"Yup," he said. "Makes a nice souvenir." He stood close to me and stuffed a brick of cash into the jacket breast pocket. He looked back beyond the piano and out the window, as though he were looking back in time. "Watch your back in this town, son."

"I have been so far," I said. "See you tonight."

There was an emptiness, maybe even regret in his eyes. His expression was like he wanted to say something. He whistled for Winston, and they walked out as a pair. Gibson continued to whistle his way down the hall.

"Hey," I said. He stopped and looked back at me. "Wrong way."

"Right."

He turned around and headed for the stairs.

Chapter Forty-three

"I really don't want to be here," I said.

Nora eased the BMW up to the Willard valet. There were two cars ahead of us. "And I do?"

We had an hour before the cocktail reception, and a lot needed to happen. The guests had been invited, but we needed them to start checking in.

"It's just a sick feeling. I can't describe it. This is as bad as it gets, in my opinion."

"I've been dealing with that feeling for four years. Do you want that tape or not?"

"I don't want it…*we* want it. We *need* it."

"So, there's your answer."

She grabbed the ticket from the valet and walked around the car. We stood outside the Willard's entrance, which included an enormous glass portico with American flags on either side. It had gone under a massive renovation in 1986 and had played host to many significant occasions through the years. And now it was about to host one of the dirtiest, most corrupt schemes imaginable.

"I wish it were that simple. But after spending an hour trying to make him leave my grandma's condo, I'm a little concerned."

"Did I miss something?"

"If coked-out Mozart qualifies, or a revolver in your face, then yes, you missed something."

Nora stopped and faced me. Behind her, the Washington Monument reflected the day's last sliver of sunshine. "Calvin," she spoke with sincerity, "I told him no Foxhall. I'm sorry."

"I shouldn't have gone back there myself. My family wasn't home, but…." I dwelled on what had happened earlier and wasn't sure if I should share everything with her just yet, like the cash. I had counted it after Gibson left: almost twelve grand. It was dirty money, and I wasn't sure what to do with it.

Nora pulled me away from the entrance, so no one would hear us. "What did you do?"

"Once he put his pistol away, I tried to get him to leave. And that's when he decided to show off on the piano. I've got to say, he sure didn't seem like a guy preparing for the biggest heist of his life."

"These things take time," she said. "There's no money exchanged tonight. We still have to pull it off and bury a few treasures, if you know what I mean."

"Whose side are you on, Nora?"

"Remember what we talked about. Until we get what we need, we're stuck." Even after her saving me at Kalorama, I was still getting mixed messages from her. If that was a slip of the tongue, I was sure of one thing: *trust no one*.

"If he fucks this up and doesn't come through with the tape. . .*our* tape," I said, "I'm going to bury a few treasures of my own."

Nora peered at me like the naïve, Midwestern boy that I was. "Just don't forget what I told you about some of these people."

She glanced at her watch and then looked up and down Pennsylvania Avenue. It dawned on me that some important players were not present: the callboys. This is where the reality hit home—the reality of what Gibson and his pack did for a living. Nora had one foot on the carpet to walk inside when a limousine pulled up and Raymond got out of the passenger's seat, glaring right at me. "At least he's punctual," she said. The back door opened and one by one, the callboys—all dressed in tuxedos—got out, most of them lighting up cigarettes. They all had the youthfulness of teenagers but with pale skin and dark circles under their eyes. Nora spoke to one of them who called on the others to follow him inside.

"Any close calls?" Raymond said. He still looked like I remembered: stout, business-like, and with dark-rimmed glasses.

"No," I said. "Not even close. Funny, we thought you might have slipped off the radar."

He shut the limo door. "Somebody had to do the dirty work."

Raymond looked around and walked inside.

"Now we just need Eli," I said. I lit a smoke even though I knew Nora wouldn't approve. "Look, I'm not reviewing any video or anything. We get these guys where we need them, and then Mark can handle the rest. Assuming this even goes off."

The doorman, in his stiff, maroon suit and brass buttons, pulled on the heavy glass door and let Nora inside. I put out my cigarette and looked down the street, wondering how and when Eli was going to show up.

Chapter Forty-four

Nightfall had arrived, and the Independence Day fireworks were being set up and tested. Nora and I had gone upstairs to check things out in the suites.

"How does he make arrangements with the callboys?" I said.

"I didn't tell you?"

"No."

She stopped and looked at me. "Then I guess that means it's none of your business."

Nora had been forthcoming about everything leading up to that night. I found it troubling that she wouldn't share how the callboys were selected and paid. She was still clinging to something.

We found both rooms to be as we'd left them: elaborate in décor, king-sized beds covered in down pillows, mini-bars, terrycloth robes, and a television facing the bed. The television gave me a chilling recollection of the day before, when Nora slid a video tape in the VCR at Gibson's condo. I had nearly become sick with the thought of what was on that tape, and now that feeling had only intensified. Other than the typical amenities, there were no signs of any guests staying overnight.

"Let's get downstairs," I said.

"What time is it?"

"Quarter to nine, why?"

"I'm concerned about Eli. His clients can become restless."

"You mean this is going down soon? This early?"

"It may. You know, you can't play cards until the dealer shows up, but two of those callboys have a room key, and apparently Eli is still at the Harrington." Eli had booked a room at Hotel Harrington on Eleventh Street so he could stay out of the picture until it was time.

"Wait," Nora said, standing at the elevator. "I almost forgot." I followed her down the hall to room 1203. She paused outside the door and looked at me. "You may want to stay out here."

"Why?"

"I'll only be a minute, Calvin."

"They're already here, aren't they?"

"I'm trying to protect you. There's something I need to verify, and you may not be welcome. Please, just wait." She pointed toward a bench in the hallway.

Fear set in as I watched Nora knock on the door. No one answered. She knocked again. I looked down the quiet hallway in both directions. Nora had her back to me when the door started to open, so I brushed past her into the room. "Calvin!"

Mark looked at both of us. "You brought the kid with you?" he said, ignoring me. He walked back through the parlor and into the master suite, not waiting for a response.

"Can you wait here at least?" she said.

"No." I walked past her and into the bedroom.

Mark held a television remote and fumbled with something on the back of the TV. "Almost ready," he said, smiling in my face. My dislike for him in our brief encounter had now turned into a deep contempt. If I called him a creep, it would've been a compliment.

Nora noticed my expression and kept things rolling. "You tested both rooms?"

"Audio and visual." Mark beamed with pride. It must be so gratifying knowing that you wired a place for blackmail. In police work, a sting is orchestrated to fight crime by catching the suspect in the act. In the underground world of Eli Gibson, there's no interest in catching anyone. When you get down to the brass tacks, the crime itself is encouraged. It's in the dirty work that follows where the villain makes his mark.

I glanced at Nora and so desperately wanted to say, *How in God's name have you lived with yourself around this madness?* Mark pushed a couple buttons on the remote, and the TV turned on. After a brief delay, we were looking at a live picture of one of the rooms. I recognized the beige and red accents on the bed and drapery. My heart shuddered, I looked for a spot to land my fist on Mark's red, clammy skin. I needed to get away from him for both of our sakes.

"Okay, anything else?" Nora said.

"Hang on, watch this." Using another remote, he switched to a different camera, "The other suite." Another sly grin closed the deal for me.

"We have to go," I said.

276

"But it's almost showtime," Mark said.

"Is that what this is to you?"

"Fuck you, kid."

Nora stepped between us. "Gentlemen."

"*Gentlemen* don't get their rocks off the way this guy does," I said. My ego needed resolve. I couldn't just walk away. I needed to see that look of shame from him knowing I knew what he was hiding. His shoulders slumped, and he avoided eye contact with us. *There it is.*

"Let's go, Calvin."

***

Once in the lobby, we were not prepared for the report of one of the mortars. The resonant *Boom!* caused me to take a step back. I exited the elevator and looked around. Several groups were gathered in the lobby, watching the Fourth of July fireworks through the vaulted windows. No Gibson anywhere.

Three of the callboys walked past us toward the elevators.

"Where are they going?" I said.

"Don't concern yourself," Nora said. "We're here for one thing and one thing only."

The reality of it all had begun to take hold of me. Growing up, my mom would say, *Always make good choices*. I hadn't done well with that so far in my young life, but I tried to face my fears and stand up for what was right. I had made many mistakes, and recently, I'd nearly gotten myself killed.

The way I was raised, I couldn't allow myself to look the other way. What was about to happen at that hotel was wrong on so many levels, and If I didn't do something about it, I would regret it for all my remaining days. "So, we just ignore what's going on around us? Look the other way, get the tape and move on with our lives? What kind of people will that make us, Nora? We can't let this happen. We'd be no better than any of them."

I sensed the pressure Nora was feeling. "We *are* no better," she said. "At least right now we're not."

I faced the crowd forming in the lobby, searching for Eli. "And if we let this happen, knowing that we could've prevented it…."

Nora lowered her head.

"I'm shutting this down," I said, "with or without you."

I noticed a tremor in her voice when she said, "Knowing Eli, there's a chance he's still in his room here. I'll go—"

"First, give me the keys."

She dug through her purse and pulled out three of the four key cards. "Try twelve-oh-one first. That's where they'll be."

"Got it."

"I'll go check on Eli. If he's there, I'll make the trade."

"You're gambling that he's arrived without anyone seeing him. Just wait."

"No, I'm going."

278

"The ledger?" I said.

"In my car."

I stood close and looked in her eyes. "It's nine-oh-five. We meet back here at nine thirty. You trade with him only if he's alone."

"I'm a big girl, Cal."

***

My fear intensified with each elevator chime. With no plan, no backup, and no weapon, I was relying on luck and a sense of duty to make right a horrible situation. It's not that I was the only one who could keep this from happening, it's that I was the only one willing and crazy enough to try.

As I approached room 1201, two things occurred to me that I had in my favor. One was the element of surprise, and two, I was stone-cold sober. To my disadvantage was the fact I didn't know what I'd find on the other side of the door.

The keycard was marked, but I needed it to work on the first try. Any sound or motion might tip someone off. A vision of my family around the table at my birthday dinner made my heart pound with pride and determination. *Tonight, they'll be proud. My troubled youth, the lying and poor judgement, the attraction to mischief and danger, I could leave it all behind by taking that first step toward better streets ahead.*

It all comes down to this.

With the keycard in the slot, I had a split second left

to walk away. My only other option would involve being on the hook with Eli Gibson, and that wasn't going to happen. I reminded myself that whatever I saw or witnessed, it was nothing I couldn't stomach. *God, give me strength.* With that, I pulled the handle down and pushed the door open with a balled fist and a raging heart.

I ran into the room and saw no one. I continued through the parlor toward the master bedroom.

"What the fuck!" said one of the callboys I'd seen in the lobby. He sprung to his feet from the bed, naked as a jaybird. A dark-haired man, probably in his thirties, was also on the bed, nearly out of his clothes. He looked familiar from one of Gibson's soirees.

"Who is this?" He spoke English but with a heavy Spanish accent. He stood up and carefully walked a teardrop mirror holding a pile of cocaine over to the desk. I took a step back.

"Stay where you are," I said. The boy slowly put his pants on and grabbed his clothes, looking around in fright.

"How do you get into my room?" the Spaniard yelled.

"Never mind. I'm here to warn you about a raid."

"You! Get the fuck out of here!"

"I leave when you leave."

"Now!"

"The FBI is here."

The callboy pinched his nose, his eyes widened from the coke. The letters F-B-I must've spooked him because he sprinted past us and was gone.

The Spaniard reached for something on the desk. It was the razor blade they had used for chalking up the lines of coke. He lunged at me, going for my neck in a slashing motion. "Fuck you, Yankee motherfucker!"

I ducked his initial strike and grabbed hold of his arm, pulling him toward me. I squeezed the top of his wrist until his hand opened. The blade hit the floor, and I stepped on it, driving a knee into the man's groin and causing him to collapse.

"Listen to me," I said. "If you stay, you'll be fucked in more ways than you think."

I finally recalled where I knew him from. "Luiz, right?" He stopped resisting and looked at me with confusion. "Luiz from the polo grounds." He didn't remember me. I eyed the ice bucket that sat on the desk. Time was slipping away, and I couldn't predict where the callboy had gone. I grabbed the ice bucket and smashed the mirror, the impact spraying shards of glass in all directions.

"Wave to the camera, Luiz."

He stepped up to the desk and studied the camera setup. A trembling spasm overtook his upper body while the whites of his eyes grew large and desperate. I was waiting to take him down again if he tried attacking. Instead, he walked in a dignified manner over to a chair and got dressed as though he were leaving for the ballet. I watched him close, waiting for him to make a move toward me. He pulled a plastic bag from his pocket and sauntered over to the desk and emptied the cocaine into the bag. I walked a few paces behind him into the parlor.

On his way out the door, he looked back and said, "I kill Eli Gibson, and I kill you too, Yankee."

Chapter Forty-five

It was critical that I find Eli before anyone else. And if the police or FBI detained him, he would never be a free man again, and I could forget about ever getting my hands on that tape. I sprinted the stairwell down to the lobby level and stood behind a column near the far end of the room, looking for Nora. I walked past the front desk with my eyes peeled. I saw the general manager, the same guy who Nora had given the thousand dollars to. He had a look of *business as usual* about him. I began to wonder just how many people were in on this con.

I ran out front of the hotel and stood under the portico. People were scattered throughout the entrance and beyond. The fireworks continued to light the sky in dazzling reds and blues. I crossed Fourteenth Street and jogged toward the National Mall. Families were sprawled out on blankets, and children ran with sparklers along the Reflecting Pool. It was just another Independence Day in the nation's capital. Most people had descended on Washington to celebrate America's birthday and to take in some fireworks and history. And one person was there to orchestrate a blackmail scheme, but he was unaware that someone had come to seek revenge.

***

I continued to stand out front, hoping it might lead me to a clue and a much-needed smoke. People continued to filter across the street and into the Mall.

The light from one of the booming fireworks turned night into day. I looked through a row of elm trees and spotted two men in a struggle. *What are the chances?* It was Oliver. He was beating Eli senseless with no signs of letting up. I had gotten within a few yards of them when Oliver produced a nickel-plated Glock and pushed Eli against an elm tree.

I charged at Oliver and slammed him to the ground. I immediately went for the gun. I held his arm down and drove a forearm under his chin. His body weakened, and I used my knee to further immobilize him, smashing him in the side. With one eye on Eli, I kicked the gun out of everyone's reach.

Now the other problem: how to get rid of Oliver so I can get what I came here for. There was also the likelihood of authorities showing up.

"You want to die tonight too?" Oliver said.

Fear had left the building. Now, I was angry. Another brilliant firework display lit up the area, and I smashed my fist into Oliver's face.

Eli had taken a seat against the elm tree, spitting up blood and fighting for breath. I couldn't leave with him until Oliver disappeared, and that couldn't happen fast enough. I grabbed the Glock. I thought of emptying it and handing it back to Oliver, but I'd done enough stupid things for one lifetime.

I stuck the pistol in my jacket. "Get the fuck out of here before I change my mind."

Oliver got to his feet. "I'll be back for my money, Eli." He gave me a long stare, like he wanted to make sure he remembered my face. I watched him limp away, holding his side and trying to shake off his ass whooping.

A pause in the fireworks created darkness. "Where's Nora?" I said.

"I was wondering the same."

He tried standing up, and I shoved him back to the ground. "Your little con went nowhere."

He had difficulty trying to speak after having the wind knocked out of him. "It'll happen. Just a matter of time."

"I just saved your ass. Now, I'm going to ask you one more time, and don't try to bullshit me. Where's the tape from Foxhall?"

"What tape from Foxhall?"

I smacked him across his chin, and he let out a childish whimper. It appeared he was done fighting, not that he ever got started.

"Where the fuck is it, Eli? I'm not leaving without that tape."

Gibson looked at the Washington Monument in wonder. He reached out like he could touch it. Tears formed in his eyes. "I did a lot for this country."

***

"Right here's fine," I said. The cab driver stopped. We were within shouting distance of the back door of the Willard's kitchen. The grand finale of the fireworks turned out to be perfect cover as everyone inside had left their stations. Taking a cab around the block to keep Eli in one piece and not get detected was one of the smarter decisions I'd made that day. It threw the cabbie for a loop, but he appreciated the fifty spot. I hustled Eli to a stairwell that led to a second-floor service elevator. His legs were giving out, and his dead weight caused quite the physical burden.

We reached the eleventh floor, and I had forgotten to make good on meeting Nora. I looked at my watch, and it was nine forty. "Fuck." I leaned him up against the wall outside his room and searched his coat pockets for the room key, "The truth will set you free, right, Mr. Gibson?"

"Right," he mumbled. Blood had stuck to his lips, and his eyelids sagged.

"Eli, if you're not telling me the truth, and the Foxhall tape isn't here, you're going to wish all you had was a bloody lip."

"My word."

"Your word? Spoken like a true lobbyist." I paused and looked at him. "Where's your thirty-eight?"

"Open the fucking door, kid. Think you're a hero? I'll make you a hero.

Chapter Forty-six

While Eli cleaned himself up in the bathroom, I couldn't help but think about the past eleven months. I arrived in Washington without any real plans. I just followed the sounds of the city; more like the city took me for a ride.

Eli Gibson was a maverick and a con, but in the beginning, I liked him. He was living in high society: adventurous and celebratory. He had *the keys to the city*, or so it seemed. There were people: fascinating, powerful people. They influenced the way I thought about politics, risk taking, and how the world worked. At night, I would lie awake and listen to Massachusetts Avenue and imagine the possibilities, causing butterflies in my stomach. I had to give something back. I owed something to this town for the debts I had incurred. The opportunities put before me by my family, especially my mom, for taking the chance of moving to Washington was the most substantial debt that I owed. I needed to give back. I had reached that age where I wasn't just responsible for myself, now I was obligated to do something with it. I swore to myself, if I could get out of the mess I was in, I would try like hell to make a difference.

Eli walked out of the bathroom and had caught a second wind. He began pushing furniture around, blocking the door with an ottoman and a leather desk chair.

"What are you doing?" I said.

"Don't want any visitors."

"The door's locked, Eli."

He popped the cork on a bottle of champagne that had been chilling. Considering his pain, it was much needed medication.

"The tape, Eli. I'm not hanging around."

He nearly fell as he opened the door of a large cedar armoire. He pulled a tape from one of the drawers and handed it to me. On it, written in black marker, was *Fox 5/21/89.*

"How do I know this is the only copy?" My voice cracked as I thought over countless scenarios of how he could manipulate the transaction. The way things were looking, he was going to wind up paying dearly for his crimes, whether he had the tapes or the ledger, or both.

He scratched his chin and looked toward the door. "Where's Miss Nora?"

"Answer my question, Eli."

Nora's absence was making matters uncertain for me. But as much as I was concerned about our trade, her safety made me nervous. I wanted to go find her. I could just imagine her on her way to the room with the ledger when one of Eli's goons stopped her.

If that were the case, she would know how to defend herself. My mind wandered into resentments that I'd been wrestling with, mostly against myself. I think one of life's cruelest tricks is being caught between good and evil, it tests one's ability to make sound moral decisions and to leave greed and ego by the wayside. Only a few get it right. So far,

I wasn't one of them.

There was a gentle knock at the door.

Please don't be a cop.

I moved the chair and ottoman that Eli had used as his makeshift barricade and looked through the peephole. I saw Nora standing there, her eyes fixed back down the hallway. She held a small black briefcase.

After opening the door, I looked in both directions to make sure she was alone.

"What on earth happened?" she said.

With my foot holding the door, I whispered, "We had a run-in with Oliver across the street." I handed her the Glock. "Secure this, would you?"

With a quick shake of the head, she put the gun in her purse. "Is he in there?"

I nodded. "Bad shape."

"I was in the lobby at nine thirty. Luiz was there, so I left before he saw me."

"Had a run-in with him too."

We entered the room and I locked the door. Eli sat slumped over on the loveseat, with a hand covering his eyes.

Nora pulled the ledger from the briefcase and handed it to me. "Did you get the tape?"

Eli was lost in a drug-induced fantasy and visibly worn out from the beating he had taken. The red mark across his face looked more like a bruise now, and the bender he'd been on didn't help his appearance.

I pulled the tape from my jacket and showed it to her. "Unless there's another one just like it somewhere, our tracks should be covered." I watched her. "Wouldn't you agree, Nora?"

She placed her mouth inches from my ear. "Calvin, if I wanted to, your picture could've already been on the back of a milk carton. I suggest thinking before you speak next time."

I had no response.

Looking at Eli, I realized he had run out of options; he wasn't going back overseas, at least that's what he had told me. Dressed in a rumpled black tuxedo, he sat there listening to Mozart's "A Little Night Music" and sipped champagne.

He stood up and looked at Nora. "Dear, could I borrow your lipstick for a moment?"

She gave me a confused look and pulled one of her lipsticks from her purse and handed it to Eli. I could only look on as he walked back to the bathroom mirror. I signaled to Nora to come to the doorway. We watched him as he took the top off the lipstick and wrote the following on the mirror:

> *Chief,*
> *Consider this my resignation*
> *effective immediately. As you always*
> *said, you can't ask others to make a sacrifice*
> *if you are not ready to do the same.*
> *Life is Duty. God Bless America.*
> *To the Willard, please forgive this inconvenience.*

He wasn't one to apologize, and the room was hardly a mess. But it's not like he was thinking right to begin with. Eli walked out of the bathroom, this time with a deliberate pace, like a phone was ringing or something. His eyes were more haunted than I'd ever seen, as though he'd been visited by a ghost. He must've seen something, because the next thing I knew, he opened the drawer of the bed's nightstand and grabbed the .38. My stomach dropped. I went for Nora. He swallowed the barrel of the gun and pulled the trigger.

"No!" Nora screamed. "No, no, no!"

Eli's head snapped back as though on a swivel. He deliberately sat down on the bed while blood rushed to the front of his mouth and out the exit wound and onto the bedspread.

He dropped the gun, and his body stiffened and then shook momentarily before going limp and rolling into a half-fetal position. His steely eyes blinked. They had a *gotcha* look to them. I held Nora tight, preventing her from seeing the body.

I had never watched a person die before. It all happened so fast. I thought of the gunshot and who may have heard it. It was just past ten o'clock. Luckily, it was the Fourth of July, and the crack from his pistol could be confused with fireworks. I felt my own tears forming as I held Nora, who was in shock and reaching for him.

"No!" She tried pulling away from me. The Lord's Prayer came to my mind, which I recited in a whisper. Erasing the suicide note wouldn't be a good idea; it would need to be documented, and I didn't want to tamper with anything.

We had to leave. I arranged the furniture to make sure the room was left the way it was originally.

Nora knelt in front of Gibson with her head down. "You need to leave right now, Calvin."

"What do you mean? You're coming with me."

"I'm staying," she said. "It has to be this way." Nora's tears began to subside. She held her face in her hands and reached for a deep breath. From the time I had met this woman, she had shown me so much. It was an apprenticeship. I would've followed her to the ends of the earth. And then it all got flipped on me. But she had saved me once. And now she's cutting me loose. When the investigation picks up again, Nora would most likely play a significant role in its outcome. Nora Dalton was the token woman, and no one knew that like I did. She was unforgettable.

I opened the door. "You sure?"

"There's no other way," she said. "I'll notify the authorities, and I'll keep you out of it. Far as they're concerned, you walked his dog."

After checking the peephole, I opened the door. "Thank you, Nora."

Drunk with fear, I was about thirty paces from the elevator, but it seemed like a city block. The swaying sensation of swimming in open waters overtook me. And I was frightened, like something was about to bite my leg. It was hard to keep my wits. I heard the elevator bell ring and the slight shake of the door, indicating an arriving car. It was too late to turn around, too late to try to hide.

Oliver.

He walked out of the elevator and sucker-punched me, knocking me back into the wall. "Where's Eli?"

"He's dead."

"Fuck you. Where is he?"

"He's gone. When are you going to realize we're on the same team, Oliver?"

"You're lying." He looked down the hall and listened intently for anything or anyone.

"I just watched Eli blow the back of his head off. I wouldn't lie about that."

"No, he didn't. He wouldn't."

"Nora's with him. She's called the authorities. We need to vanish."

"Why should I trust you?" He began pacing.

"That's you in the picture on the bar at Foxhall, isn't it?"

He glared at me. "I was twelve."

"You're his son?"

"He just always called me that. Told people he adopted me."

I know the feeling. I took a step toward the elevator and reached for the button when Oliver grabbed my hand. "Let's use the stairs."

We reached the lobby level and hadn't said a word to each other. But I had one more question. Considering I would never have an experience like this again in my life, I wanted to know the whole story behind Eli Gibson and his secret enterprise. "Were you supposed to be in on this tonight? Or was there something else?"

"Isn't there always something else?"

I stood by the lobby door as he rounded the stairwell. "Were you going to kill him?"

He reached for a deep breath and gripped the stairwell railing. "I'm not sure," he said. "I wanted to. And he deserved to die."

"Why?"

He broke out a cigarette and tapped it against his hand. "Broken promises."

I watched him walk down the stairs. It was hard not to think that he was also a survivor. Just like Nora and countless others. I took the hallway down toward the Round Robin Bar and exited out onto Fourteenth Street. I needed a drink, but it wouldn't be there.

Gibson was dead. That much I knew. But his story was just beginning—for the press anyway. I thought for a moment what my uncle might have to say. When it came to Jack Gregory, I had but one option: to come clean. It's hard to lie to a man who lives on a street named *Honesty Way*.

***

In a perfect world, Nora and I could've taken in the fireworks from one of the best views in the city: the rooftop of Foxhall. Instead, I was alone on that clear, beautiful night. I stood in wonder, staring out at that *Shining City upon a Hill*, as President Reagan often said. While tourists had taken in the patriotic festivities of Independence Day, I took in a suicide, one that came with a trail of mysteries never to be solved. The fireworks of Eli's conspiracy left a mark that, God willing, would help fight similar crimes in the future, and his grand finale at the Willard would stay with me for the rest of my life.

Instead of dreaming about the possibilities that this town had etched in granite, I saw empty promises, corruption, lies, and strong-arming. It was all masked by the glamour and show that Eli Gibson was so good at delivering, yet the ship he sailed was something he knew would never come into port. Originally, succeeding in Washington seemed to be about good marks and honest work, all the things I had heard repeatedly from my family. The thing that I had got wrong, more than anything else, was that I wanted it *now*.

For Nora and me, there would be no accolades or promises. No awards and certainly no applause. Instead, we had a full-blown scandal on our hands, and now we had a body.

I looked toward the Jefferson Memorial, and the wind pulled the smoke from my lips. I thought of Nora offering a sly look across a room at me, maybe she pulls her hair back and places her wine glass on a piano and walks away. It's an invitation. That's just it: it's a symbol for an open invitation. The same kind I fell headfirst into. I imagined the dome of the Jefferson with a crack in it, about the size of the one on my heart.

Have you seen enough now?

Eli Gibson's demons won the battle that he had wrestled with for so long. Had he chosen otherwise, a lengthy stay in prison for countless crimes would've awaited him: extortion, sex trafficking, blackmail, racketeering, prostitution, and fraud to name a few. Considering his name was forever tarnished in Washington, it appeared he had seen enough. His choice was a cowardly one, but the alternative would've been more than he could bear. To grow up Eli Gibson, with lofty dreams in media, politics, and public service, only to discover being different and that you'd be stigmatized and discriminated against for being so, it must've weighed heavily on his mind and spirit.

And so, he chose a life of crime.

His long, downward spiral must've started when he realized he'd never fulfill the dream of ambassadorship like his idol, Perle Mesta. No, he would instead go down in a blaze of shame and humiliation.

In the end, Gibson knew the jig was up. His story ended in another random hotel room. He had betrayed and cheated so many along the way, not even the ledger could keep tally. He *wanted a seat at the table,* as he'd once said, and he was willing to do anything to exploit those who he thought were standing in his way. Eli Gibson never wanted to be the bad guy—it just kind of worked out that way.

ABOUT THE AUTHOR

While pursuing a career in veterans advocacy, Mr. Smith has developed and maintained a blog about mental health since 2013. A U.S. Army veteran, T.R. lives in Cleveland, Ohio, and The Age of Majority is his first novel. When not writing, he tries to get outdoors, or in front of a menu, the backyard grill or a cigar with friends, or to bargain with his two rescue pets that run his household.

ABOUT DONATIONS TO BBRF

Ten percent of each book sale will be donated to a cause that will continue to form the author's platform for giving back. The Brain & Behavior Research Foundation is a 501c non-profit organization with headquarters in New York City. BBRF awards grants to scientists around the world who are committed to finding cures for mental illness. The donors and supporters of the foundation are committed to alleviating the suffering of those who live with various forms of mental illness. 100% of all donations to BBRF goes to research. This is possible because of the generous support of two different family foundations that cover its operating expenses. Those facts alone made choosing BBRF an easy decision. You can learn more about the foundation at https://www.bbrfoundation.org Donations will be made quarterly and progress updates will be made on the author's website at http://www.trsmithauthor.com/

"To think too much is a disease." – Fyodor Dostoyevsky

68242583R00186

Made in the USA
Columbia, SC
05 August 2019